lulu in LA LA LAND

BY ELISABETH WOLF

sourcebooks
jabberwocky

Published by Sourcebooks Jabberwocky, an imprint of Sourcebooks, Inc.
P.O. Box 4410, Naperville, Illinois 60567-4410
(630) 961-3900
Fax: (630) 961-2168
www.jabberwockykids.com

Library of Congress Cataloging-in-Publication data is on file with the publisher.

Source of Production: Versa Press, East Peoria, Illinois, USA
Date of Production: May 2013
Run Number: 20512

Printed and bound in the United States of America.
VP 10 9 8 7 6 5 4 3 2 1

To:
William and Beverly Bierer
(who we call Gammy and Papa)

Prologue:

Lulu's Beginning

ME

My mom, dad, and sister suspect that I'm from another planet. They believe that I'm the Alien Child. I'm sure of it. My family is glamorous. The Harrisons are Hollywood royalty at its best, except for me. I've got massively different ideas on how life should be.

My name is Lulu Harrison, daughter of the super cool actor Lincoln Harrison and famous film director Fiona. I'm little sister to fashionable, fancy fifteen-year-old Alexis. My address is 15000 Stone Canyon Road, Bel Air, California (that area between Beverly Hills and Brentwood).

You'd think my life was pampering and parties. Well, it could be, but the problem is, I'm the Not Fitter Inner. I love to garden. The rest of my family loves to groom. I love to bake. They love to buy. I love science experiments. They love strenuous exercise (like yoga or Pilates). Are you starting to understand?

MY FAMILY

Here's what it means to be a Not Fitter Inner.

Everyone who ever meets my dad or reads about him thinks he's dreamy. They're not wrong. He's got thick, wavy brown hair and forest-green eyes. BUT I have this secret idea he doesn't even know where my room is in the house. I'm one gazillion percent sure he doesn't know the name of my best friend, my favorite food, or what grade I'm in.

My mom is tall, thin, and beautiful. Sometimes she can be the warmest, kindest mom on the planet. But most of the time she's distracted. Being a director, she's used to bossing people around and making sure everything around her is perfect. I don't try to act anything like perfect, and I sure don't want to be bossed around.

My sister, Alexis, is flaw free, or at least that's what she's always telling me. She has thick, dark hair that's always blown out. She has an L.A.-style toothpick body. People constantly mistake her for a young actress. She loves that beyond belief.

Here's how I look: plain. I have frizzy, shapeless brown hair that I never have time to cut or brush. I've got pale skin with overlapping freckles. I'm average height and just a little teeny-tiny bit extra chunky. I sure don't want to look like those walking skeletons you see around L.A. My best feature on the outside is my deep-green eyes. My other best parts that you can't see, like my brain and my feelings, my family doesn't care about. Out of sight, out of mind.

THE REAL LULU

In case you secretly believe being a kid in this family is easy, forget it! Here's what being different means:

1. Whenever I get stuck going to boring stores with Alexis, I accidentally spray myself with room freshener, thinking it's perfume. She laughs at me.
2. Even though Alexis commands me to get a two-piece bathing suit, I can never find one that works. Either the top fits and the bottom doesn't, or the bottom fits and the top doesn't. So, I only wear one-piece suits. Alexis laughs at me.
3. I bring a book to movie premieres. If the movie seems stupid, I sneak-read with an orange clip-on book light. My mother gets mad and sends me out of the theater. Alexis laughs at me.
4. My mere existence makes Alexis laugh at me, like I'm a walking joke.

Here's who I truly am: that white iris that pops up in the thick, beautiful garden of all purpley-blue ones. That's really a famous Vincent Van Gogh painting. It hangs in the nearby Getty Museum. I'm the flower that just came up the wrong color, but the truth is that painting wouldn't be a masterpiece if it wasn't for the white iris. If Van Gogh just painted all blue and purple irises, zillions of people over the last hundred years would walk by that painting and say, "Nice goopy brush strokes. Very pretty," and then they'd shuffle past. But that white iris makes people stop and stare, and absolutely, positively know they're looking at a *grande* masterpiece.

THE NEW LULU

In one month, it's going to be my eleventh birthday. I'm planning the most *fantastico* party. There's something about double digits—well, real double digits. I mean, that zero next to the one in ten, is, well, zero. It doesn't count. Those tall, straight ones, side by side, have a real meaning, like standing up for who you are. Eleven will be my Best Year Ever! The Harrisons will understand that I'm an important, creative, spectacular member of this family.

Because I live in Hollywood, I'm going to document my story by writing my own screenplay. This is it: *Lulu in LA LA Land*. I've never actually written a script before, but everyone in L.A. does (even our dog nanny and pool dude).

Most of all, my parents live, breathe, eat, and work in a world created by scripts. Movie scripts are what my parents read more than anything else. Why not take a shot at one?

So, here goes…

LULU IN LA LA LAND

BY LULU HARRISON

Based On: My Life
Lulu Harrison
1500 Stone Canyon Road
Bel Air, California 90077
Lulu@LuluinLALALand.com
© 2013

ACT I: PLANNING MAKES PERFECT?

SCENE 1: SAVE THE CILANTRO

EXT. HARRISON ESTATE GROUNDS, GARDEN— SATURDAY MORNING

 CUT!! Since this is the first screenplay I've ever written and might be the first screenplay you've ever read, here's some script stuff I wanna explain. Before each scene, I'll show where it takes place by putting "EXT.," which means whatever is gonna happen is gonna happen outside (exterior), or "INT.," which tells ya what's gonna happen is gonna be inside (interior). Easy, right? OK, back to: ACTION!!

EXT. FADE IN ON:

The morning sun shines brightly on rows of wilted cilantro plants. LULU, an almost eleven-year-old girl with long, unruly brown hair, stands covered in garden soil, frantically examining her garden. ELANA, a middle-aged Latina with bunned black hair and warm brown eyes, stands patiently, trying to reason with Lulu. Elana wears khakis and a light blue cotton sweater. No-nonsense clothes for her no-nonsense way.

LULU

There must be something wrong, because every leaf is wilting and the dirt is bone dry.

ELANA

Just get the hose and water it. I help you.

WATSON, the Harrisons' chubby pug, waddles up to sniff around the plants.

LULU

I've gotta find Hernandez. I think he's here. His crew's still here.

ELANA

We never gonna find Hernandez. He could be anywhere on the property. We'll get a hose.

LULU

No gracias, Elana. We can't just yank out the hose and water. Ya know there's a drought, and we're only supposed to water on Tuesdays and Thursdays before eight in the morning. And the whole reason Hernandez invented the solar-powered drip system is so I don't waste water.

ELANA

Niña, Lulu, you wanna have cilantro, tomatoes, onions, and chilies for the salsa you make for your birthday fiesta, you better grab the hose.

LULU
(waving her hand around)
He's gotta be here somewhere.

ELANA

Hernandez cannot make rain, and if he's here, he's gotta make the flowers and big bushes look nice for your parents.

 CUT!! I just have to break in here for a quick sec and tell you something about Elana. I call her my "Momny." That's "mommy" and "nanny" together. Elana's heart is bigger than North and South America combined. When I'm sick with fever, she hugs me like she's never heard of germs. When I get scared, she speaks to me like she doesn't notice. There are times when I make her crazy, like probably right now, but she doesn't let on. OK, back to: ACTION!!

LULU

It's my birthday, Elana. Salsa's my *favorita*. I want to make the best batch ever, and I want it all to be from my garden. This is really important!

Lulu gives Elana's hand a squeeze as she heads off running down a hilly slope. She darts past the swimming pool and cabana, past the tennis court, herb garden, and rose beds, toward the edge of the

Harrisons' estate where ten-foot-high pittosporum plants border the property. The chunky pug tries to follow Lulu but lies down exhausted after a few feet. He'd much rather play dead than chase.

SCENE 2: STOP THAT CAR AND DRIVER!

EXT. HARRISON ESTATE GROUNDS, FRONT GATE—CONTINUOUS

Lulu arrives at the front gate of the property, panting and out of breath. She looks in the direction of buzzing, motorized cutters. The sound comes from the tops of ladders propped against the giant hedges.

LULU
(yelling over the roar)
HERNANDEZ?! ARE YOU UP THERE? IT'S GONNA BE MY BIRTHDAY, AND I WAS GONNA MAKE SALSA FOR MY PARTY, BUT MY CILANTRO PLANTS ARE WILTING!

 CUT!! Just so you know why I'm searching everywhere for Hernandez. He keeps all the leaves, blades of grass, petals of flowers, and tree branches looking ready for a garden magazine photo shoot. His dark, soft eyes look at me the most kind and patient way—no matter how many questions I ask about watering, seeds, sunlight, bugs, or organic fertilizer. Back to: ACTION!!

                    WORKER IN TREE
Hernandez's not up here.

                         LULU
                    (still yelling)
GRACIAS! DO YOU KNOW WHERE HE IS?

As Lulu bellows into the tops of the hedges, a pearl-white hybrid
Escalade glides silently into the Harrison motor court, through
open gates then up the long cobblestone driveway.

INT. ESCALADE—CONTINUOUS

PETAL, the driver, LINCOLN, the father, FIONA, the mother,
and ALEXIS, the sister, all silently look out tinted glass windows,
the kind you can see out but no one can see in. Each of the
occupants notices Lulu with her hands cupped to her mouth,
bellowing into the thick bushes.

Alexis looks at her parents and rolls her eyes.

EXT. MOTOR COURT—CONTINUOUS

Noticing the car as it passes her on the driveway, Lulu tears off
in the direction of the moving vehicle. She waves her hands and
arms in an enormous and obvious effort to stop the car.

                         LULU
                     (shouting)
PETAL, PETAL, CAN YOU STOP? MOM, DAD, ARE YOU
IN THERE?

The Escalade pulls into the motor court, stopping in front of the house. A window glides down. Petal sticks her arm out and makes a peace sign.

> PETAL
> (out the window to Lulu)
> Don't worry. I see you, babe.

Lulu reaches the car. She's covered in garden soil and breathless from her loopy running.

> LULU
> Mom! Dad! Are you in there?

Lulu sticks her head into the open car window, talking as fast as the words can tumble out.

> LULU
> Hi! How was Santa Barbara? Are you home for a while now? I've got a big problem. Well, ummmmm, the problem is part of a surprise I wanna do for my birthday. I really need help finding Hernandez to fix the water dripper so the cilantro doesn't die!

As she runs out of breath, Lulu's voice sputters to a halt. Linc has a slight soft drawl to his deep, smooth voice.

> LINC
> (charmingly mocking himself)
> Darling, that's a lot of lines for an actor like me who can

only memorize a sentence at a time. I'm still at the "Hi," and I want to say "Hi" back, and "I missed you," and give ya a hug.

Linc exits the car and wraps his arms around Lulu. Fiona unfolds her long, lean self from the other side and joins the two, smoothing Lulu's wild hair in an automatic, motherly way.

FIONA
(jokingly)
I see you've been taking care of yourself while I've been gone.

LULU
I have, Mom. I've been doing lots of cooking with Elana. I'm planning my birthday party and—

Alexis stands in front of the house.

ALEXIS
About that party! Not sure what dying plants have to do with a birthday party, but you're totally off track.

LULU
I don't want to tell you everything because I was going to surprise you guys.

FIONA
Surprise us now, Lu. You wanted our help with something when we pulled up.

LULU
(rapid fire)
Oh, geez peas! OK. Well, for my birthday, I wanna invite you all to dinner with Elana and my forever best friend, Sophia. I'm gonna make you all personal invitations from pressed flowers. I'm gonna decorate the table with homegrown garden flowers. Sophia and I already designed party hats. And, I'm gonna cook! Everything! A to Z, but, well, nothing I'm making starts with A or Z. My menu's gonna be: homemade chips and spicy salsa. All the salsa ingredients are growing in my organic garden. That's where the big problem comes in because the water—

ALEXIS
(cuts in)
The whole idea is the Big Problem! Look, you already lost me at the hat designing part. And what about those two?

Alexis glances towards Linc and Fiona who bicker in whispers a few feet away.

ALEXIS
They don't seem too excited about handmade garden flowers.

LULU
Homegrown.

ALEXIS
(thrusting her chin their parents' direction)
Whatever. Just look at them.

Lulu turns toward her parents. Linc and Fiona carry on their own sharp conversation. When they realize the girls are watching, they stop. Linc saunters over to Lulu and drapes his strong arm around her shoulder.

LINC
(oozing charm)
Like I said, I'm just a not-too-bright actor. So, I'm still stuck on my first line, "Hi, Santa Barbara rocked."

Lulu opens her mouth to respond, but her mother is already yelling.

FIONA
Linc, stop with that not-smart stuff! You get a few unflattering reviews, and you believe you're not a smart, thoughtful, inspiring man of your craft. I cannot stand it! I'm never casting you again because I can't handle you off the screen.
(then, in a soft tone to Lulu.)
I'm going inside, Lu, to stretch out after the long car ride.

Linc slinks back into the car. Windows go up.

PETAL
Hey, Lulu, I'm for you!

Petal gives Lulu a thumbs up as she maneuvers the huge white car out of the Harrison estate gates.

SCENE 3: FANCIER IS MORE FABULOUS

EXT. HARRISON ESTATE, POOLSIDE—SAME DAY

Lulu and Alexis are having lunch at an iron table between the cabana and the pool. The nearby pool house is a smaller version of the main house. The Olympic-sized infinity pool (one without edges) gleams in the sunlight. The water is always hyperclean, thanks to the pool dude, CHIP, who cleans the pool. He wears baggy black board shorts and a faded ZJ Board Shop T-shirt.

As Lulu and Alexis eat, Watson mills about their feet, lapping up food from the floor. A soggy, baggy diaper hangs loosely from his back haunches.

> ALEXIS
> That smelly dog is like a vacuum—he sucks up everything he can get his tongue on. Can't we eat in peace?! I can't believe Fiona lets you keep this beast.

> LULU
> Watson's allowed anywhere with his diaper, so *por favor* live with it.

Watson licks around Lulu's chair.

> LULU
> Look, the puggy even likes the spicy stuff.

ALEXIS
Your sandwiches ooze. They're always dripping
something red like they're bleeding to death.

LULU
Does that mean you don't want a bite?

Lulu lifts her leaking sandwich and waves it in Alexis's direction.
Plops of tomato salsa hit the table and Lulu's leg.

ALEXIS
Don't even swing that drippy mess near me.

LULU
And for your information, it's salsa squished in grilled
cheese. My own recipe. I've been trying out different
salsas to make for my birthday. There's hot, super-duper
hot, medium-mild—

ALEXIS
You mean that Little Chef Lulu Nature Hugger party?
Not happening. That's like for a hippy-dippy eco baby.

LULU
Being four and three-quarters years younger than you
doesn't make me a baby.

ALEXIS
For your birthday, let's grow you up.
(thinks for a beat)
I know! How about a premiere party? I'll check

soon-to-be-released blockbuster movies. Fiona's assistant
can get a print of one, and I'll screen it at the house. I
could get about thirty girls into our downstairs theater.
I'll get popcorn buckets with your name on—

LULU
(interrupting)
Lex, I don't like blockbuster movies. And I don't have
thirty girlfriends.

ALEXIS
OK. Next.
(thinks for a milli-moment)
Got it! Disco dance party. I'll set up an outside dance
floor. Fiona has done that tons of times here. I'll score a
hot DJ. I'll check out who just did Amanda Sasson's hot
shots party last weekend. That DJ rocked.

LULU
I wasn't there.

ALEXIS
Well, everyone who matters was there.

CHIP
I was there.

Chip has been listening in on the conversation as he pushes a
long sweeper across the length of the pool's bottom.

ALEXIS
(calls out to Chip)
You were? But you're, well, a little older than the crowd that was there.

CHIP
(in a flat, relaxed tone)
Working extra jobs. Surfing's an expensive habit. Besides cleaning pools, I pass around appetizers for a caterer. Ya know, all that time riding a board, I've got balance. I can hold two trays of soy-encrusted cucumber and pick up dirty plates at the same time.

LULU
Mega yuck! What's soy crusty cucumber like?

 CUT!! Gotta tell you something funny about Chip. He's nut-o about eating a strict vegetarian diet. But I swear on a stack of cookbooks that I once saw him on Venice Beach eating a hot dog. I've never mentioned it to anyone, not even him, because, geez peas, what's so awful about a little hot dog here and there…and, besides, I'd never want to embarrass him. Back to: ACTION!!

LULU
(to Alexis)
Doesn't Robbie surf?
(to Chip)
He's her new boyfriend.

ALEXIS
(annoyed)
Can we get back to the party business?

CHIP
How 'bout a pool party? I'll make sure there's not a bee's wing in the water. I'll skim it crystal clear.

ALEXIS
Thanks, Chip, but, no! Pool party is way overdone.

Alexis faces Lulu, up close and personal.

ALEXIS
Lulu, what fab parties have YOU been to lately?

LULU
(voice trails off)
Well, you know...

ALEXIS
No, I don't. That's why I'm asking.

LULU
I don't go to many parties, Lex. Just not invited too much. And it's fine because I wouldn't want to go.

ALEXIS
That's just weird of you.

LULU

Wait, I did just go to the greatest Easter party. Sophia
and her mom invited me, and we painted giant chocolate
eggs with colored icing.

ALEXIS

'K, halt! Not getting anywhere. Slam on the brakes.

LULU

I have a birthday party planned. Geez peas! Sophia's
gonna come and Elana...and Chip!
(calling out to Chip)
You should come too. And, Lex, believe it or not, I want
you if you can slide me into your social schedule. And
Robbie, if you guys are still going out. And most of all,
Mom and Dad, and that's—

ALEXIS

(interrupting)
Your problem! You're NOT, NO WAY going to get Linc and
Fiona to a make-your-own-taco birthday dinner. They're
too busy. It's gotta be a smashy-flashy party that they
WANT to attend. Lulu, you throw parties that are fun for
your guests!

Lulu is unable to respond for a minute. Alexis's words sting
her ears.

LULU

It's not a make-your-own-taco party! I wanted to make
garden-grown, homemade salsa. I wanted to make mini

pizzas. I wanted to make mac and cheese from scratch. I wanted—

ALEXIS

Linc and Fiona to come, right?

LULU
(very quietly)
Yes.

ALEXIS

Got it, gal. Gonna take this one over. I'll be your party planner.

RING TONE MUSIC BLARES. It's Alexis's phone. Alexis answers.

ALEXIS
(into phone, animated)
Oooooh, fabby that you called to remind me! I'll get driven right over.

Alexis disconnects and slips her feet into her leopard print slide thong sandals. Her salad's barely touched.

ALEXIS
(to Lulu)
Nail appointment. Mani-pedi.

Realizing that she's about to make a quick getaway, Alexis musters a tiny stab of kindness for her little sister.

18

ALEXIS

Wanna come?

Lulu looks at her salsa-damp fingertips. She unconsciously stuffs them through her wildly messy hair, which hasn't been brushed since dashing around this morning.

LULU

Not my thing, Lex, but gracias for asking.

A moment of inspiration flashes over Alexis. It may have come as she watched Lulu spread salsa through her hair or when she worried that her own nails might not be cleaned, buffed, filed, and polished as scheduled.

ALEXIS

It WILL be your thing! Spa party! Fab-u-lous. Nails, hair, massage, waxing, facials. The works. EVERYONE demands, requires, craves beauty treatment. And HELLO?! Where are Linc and Fiona always dashing off to besides the set or the studio? Some grooming appointment, that's what!

LULU

I always thought primping was just part of their work.

ALEXIS

Get with the program, Lu. Everyone in L.A. loves to looks great. It's not a job! It's a duty!

LULU
I don't know anyone who would want to come to that kind of party. Well, except maybe you, Mom, and Dad.

ALEXIS
Guest list. I'm on it. I'll get your school directory and the Harrison family holiday card list and get cracking.

Alexis stands and grabs her purple Chanel purse.

ALEXIS
By the way, HELLLLLO?! You just said it yourself. Your PARENTS would want to go to THIS kind of party.

Alexis turns on her high heels but halts. Both girls smell the odor. Looking under the table, they find Watson, minus his diaper. He's just made a giant poop and is now eating the steaming pile.

Alexis screams in horror.

ALEXIS
I hate that awful dog! What's WRONG with him? He's totally defective.

LULU
(defiant while holding her nose)
I love puggy. Just think of him as the ultimate recycler!

Alexis, totally grossed out, runs away. But before she's out of earshot, Alexis shouts back toward Lulu.

ALEXIS
You better realize if I throw this party for you, you'll be
soooo lucky!

SCENE 4: FABULOUS
IS COSTLY

INT. ATTIC—LATER THAT SATURDAY AFTERNOON

 CUT!! Gotta break in here again to tell you about where I live. The Harrison house seems like a palace that most girls would dream about living in. Just not me. Nothing's fun about living in a place where the rules are: No touching. No scuffing. No running. No moving stuff. No leaving so much as a pencil, seed, or crumb…anywhere.

Our house is GINORMOUS. It's hard to find my family—on the rare occasion that they're home. We have an intercom phone system. I can't remember when Mom or Dad has ever answered it.

Here's what my mother's tooty-snooty decorator put in our house: lots of white and cream furniture. Lots of expensive English and French antique lamps and paintings. Nothing in my house, except in my bedroom, is for sitting with your legs up. Alexis and I are not allowed to keep any of our stuff around. Everything goes up into our rooms or into my attic playroom where nobody goes, except for me and my BFF, Sophia. Who wants to live in a place where you can't put down a glass of chocolate milk? Where I live is more of a museum than a house. Back to: ACTION!!

The attic above Lulu's room has been converted to part playroom, part creative art space. Remnants of Lulu's childhood fill the room: dolls, stuffed animals, wood blocks, a bubble-gum-pink Barbie oven, a plastic orange microscope, and a talking globe. A mobile of fairies hangs from the short ceiling. There's a craft table, two chairs, paints, clay, colored paper, and markers. A flower press sits atop a bookcase loaded with books.

SOPHIA is smaller and thinner than Lulu, even though they are both ten. She looks just like her mother, Eve, who moved to America from Japan when she was eight.

As the girls sort recipe cards into alphabetical order, Watson sleeps in an old baby doll cradle. He's swaddled in a clean diaper.

> **SOPHIA**
> My problem with making up recipes is the math. You can handle fractions and cups and liters and centi-milliliters like it's reading a book.

> **LULU**
> Cooking's just a science experiment you can eat. That makes the math part fun.

> **SOPHIA**
> Lu, I kinda want to make up a recipe by myself.

> **LULU**
> Hey, we make up all our recipes together. I always help with the measuring equations.

Sophia picks up a pencil and doodles. She stares at the paper as she talks.

SOPHIA

Truth: It's for YOU! I want to make you a birthday cake. I'm just telling you so you don't make it yourself. It's gonna be one of my presents, OK?

Sophia taps her pencil. Something's on her mind.

SOPHIA

I'm working really hard on the recipe. My mom promised she'd buy the ingredients double so I can bake it one time before I bring it. I...ummmmm...don't want it to be disgusting for your parents.

A thunderbolt strikes Lulu! The Spa Bash, now under Alexis's control, doesn't seem like the kind of party for homemade anything. For weeks, however, Sophia has been helping Lulu plan the invitations, menu, decorations, and party favors.

LULU

Geez peas! That's soooo sweet, but you and your mom shouldn't do all that.

Lulu walks over to the cradle where Watson sleeps and rocks it...faster and faster. Watson opens an eye and growls.

LULU

Really, Soph! Elana and I were gonna maybe kinda do a

cake. And, besides, seriously NO presents because you know there's nothing I need! We said...
                    (now on firmer footing)
We PROMISED when we were, what, like six years old, that we'd never give each other gifts.

Lulu runs out of "Uh-oh, how-do-I-fix-this" energy. She even stops rocking the cradle. It swings to a stop.

SOPHIA
No, Lu. What we swore on a mini-mountain of rose petals was that we'd never BUY each other presents. We always make each other presents. Remember, last Christmas, I knitted you a scarf with all those loose stitches? And you grew me that red and white candy-striped amaryllis bulb? You felt awful because at Christmas there wasn't even a flower bud.

LULU
But that was Christmas.

SOPHIA
And this is a birthday.

LULU
All I'm saying is: being eleven means I am an official tweenager.

SOPHIA
                    (quietly, now hurt and confused)
I think all you're saying is you don't want me to make your birthday cake.

(thinks a beat)
Is it because it could come out disgusting and your
parents won't like it? That's OK, Lu, I want you to have
a really good party for them.

Lulu melts inside. Her stomach feels like it will never be hungry
again. That's always where her nervous confusion ends up...in her
stomach. Lulu rubs her left hand over her belly button, thinking
she can somehow calm her swirling insides.

LULU

It's not that. I mean, it's like...well, you know, last year
they were in Africa making the *Silver Water* movie? I
absolutely, positively, one hundred percent understood
why they couldn't be with me. Year before, they were...
ummm, well, they were busy that year too.

SOPHIA

My father's never, ever been to my birthday...not even
the first one. So, Lu, I get it. I'll do anything to help you
make this birthday great so your parents like it.

LULU

Really, you'd help me?

SOPHIA
(laughing)
I'll swear on a mini-mountain of rose and daisy petals.
C'mon outside!

Lulu leans over to hug her best buddy and sees that Sophia has been scribbling pictures of fancy-looking cakes with the words, "Happy Birthday, BFF."

Silver Water

SCENE 5: Sweet and Sour

INT. CROSSWINDS SCHOOL, SCIENCE CLASS— TUESDAY

CUT!! Hey, it's me, Lulu, and I've gotta break in here to tell you about school. We all have to go. I don't care who you are, where your school is, or if it's all girls or all boys. The experience can be massively scary. Here's what I learned about school when I was in first grade: no matter what's different about you, kids are going to pick on that very thing. If you're brainy, a little pudgy, or bad at sports (and it just so happens I'm all those things) you're gonna get teased. I decided that all the parts of me that are different are great. So, why hide them? But nothing makes being different feel safe like having one supreme best friend like Sophia. Back to: ACTION!!

MR. LING, the science teacher, smiles, making his baby face look even younger. He's tall and thin as a bamboo stalk with gobs of uncombed black hair that defy gravity at all angles around his head.

MR. LING
(to students)
This is my favorite class of the week: Kids Teach Today, K.T.T. So, who's going to start? Three to five minutes on any science subject.

LULU
I'll start!

JADE
(under her breath)
Yeah. And never stop.

Kids around JADE, a leader of the popular girls, snicker.

MR. LING
Thank you, Lulu, but I remember you started last Thursday. C'mon, class. Your presentation can enhance your grade.

SAM

I'll go!

Sam bolts up from his seat in the back of the classroom and heads up front.

SAM

I wanna tell you guys about geckos and how they regenerate. That means grow back.

Sam flashes a giant smile. He's clearly into his subject.

SAM

Geckos can drop their tail. It's really cool. Their tail's long and pointy on the end, and predators can easily grab a gecko by it. But that doesn't mean he's done for! Gecko Dude can make his tail fall right off and give the bad guy the total slip!

KIDS THROUGHOUT THE CLASS

Cool! WOW!!

LULU

And it grows back! Right? That's the regeneration part.

POP GIRLS, the coolest, most stylish trendsetters of fifth grade, glance at each other. Sophia catches them and gives them a good long stare.

SAM

Yeah. And when it comes off, it doesn't bleed or anything. The muscles inside the tail just, like, squeeze it off!

Sam plays a slide show of tailless geckos on the class SMART Board.

Next FRANCES FRANK takes the podium and talks about earthquakes. He's actually shaking, though. Nerves, not an earthquake.

> FRANCES
> (reading from note cards)
> It's totally true. There are almost one million earthquakes a year. Most are little tremors, so we don't even feel them.

> JADE
> (calling across room)
> Earthquakes are such a bummer! So NOT the best part of L.A.

Jade throws Frances off. Frances freezes.

> LULU
> (looking at Frances)
> Don't most earthquakes happen underwater?

Frances scrapes up a bit of confidence, shuffles through his note cards, and continues.

> FRANCES
> Yeah. That's right. Ninety percent, actually. And that's because of the Ring of Fire.

> JANA
> Isn't that some R-rated movie?!

The class twitters. Pop Girls decide they need more attention than Kids Teach Tuesday can offer them.

LULU
(jumping in to help Frances)
It's really a chain of volcanoes that's like a gigantic upside down U in the Pacific Ocean.

FRANCES
Yeah! That's right. Seventy-five percent of all active and non-active volcanoes are in the Ring of Fire.

JANA
(to her pals)
Do you totally feel like you're watching some boring show you can't get off your screen?

Frances wraps up quickly. Since no one else is prepared to go, Lulu jumps in.

LULU
You'd think that lemon trees are from California, but they're not.

JANA
Sour topic! Shocking.

LULU
(plowing ahead)
Lemon trees aren't native to our state because a NATIVE plant is one that evolved here over a massive

long time, like even before European settlers came. Actually, Christopher Columbus brought the first lemon seeds to the New World.

Lulu talks super fast, scarcely pausing for breath.

> LULU
>
> Ya see, California Indians weren't eating or cooking lemons. Lemon trees need to be soaked with water once a week and never dry out. So, even though California has the right weather for lemon trees, 'cause it's NEVER too cold, there's not enough rain.

> SOPHIA
> (calls out)

EUREKA!!

No one understands. The class looks at Sophia blankly, like she's some freak. Lulu, however, looks at Sophia and immediately understands. She'd better hurry up. She's losing her classmates' attention.

> LULU
>
> Right! Eureka! That's not only what the California miners yelled when they struck gold, but it's the name of the lemon that grows all over our state just about all year. It's a pretty hearty tree that grows up to fifteen feet.

> SOPHIA
> (cutting in)
> And, now, Lulu has some lemon treats!

Lulu realizes what Sophia means. The Pop Girls make pucker faces, and kids around them giggle.

Lulu dashes behind the classroom door, where three big coolers sit. Each has LULU HARRISON printed across the top. Lulu drags each one to the front of the class.

> LULU
>
> Lemons are used in every kind of food, from fish to dessert. SO...
> (pauses, panting from pulling the coolers)
> Sophia and I made fresh lemonade and my own frosted lemon bars. All from Eureka lemons!

Kids tumble from their seats and crowd around Lulu. The Pop Girls, however, stay at their desks.

> JANA
>
> CAL-or-ies!!

Lulu doesn't hear because of all the jostling to get lemon treats. Sophia helps Lulu pour the lemonade.

> LULU
> (to Sophia)
> Soph, without you I'd never have gotten to the sweet from sour!

FADE OUT on Lulu and Sophia smiling at each other.

SCENE 6: TAKING A STAB AT IT

INT. BRIGHT BLUE PRIUS—EVENING

Elana and Lulu have just picked up Alexis from Robbie's house. She went home from school with him so they could do online research on L.A.'s best spa treatments. Alexis reports on her spa brainstorming session while searching the web on her iPhone for more ideas.

Driving by Mr. Chow, a fancy restaurant in Beverly Hills, they see Petal parked outside. That means Linc and Fiona must be inside having dinner.

Lulu wears her standard uniform—a surf T-shirt, a bright orange skirt, an orange crocheted scarf around her neck, and her personalized checkerboard Vans. Lulu colors the shoes' white squares orange using a magic marker. Orange is her absolute favorite color.

> LULU
>
> Please, Elana! Let's pull in for a sec, a flash, a nano-moment! Lex, tell them about the spa party. If you think it's gonna be great, let's tell them right now. I wanna make sure they know and don't go anywhere else that day.

> ALEXIS
>
> Why don't I wait till I have details planned? Hellllo?! I need to make lots of arrangements here. I don't even

have invitations, a date, or a time. It's zippo the hippo at the moment...well, except for my one Grand Plan.

LULU

A Grand Plan is a good place to start. C'mon, Lex! If it's such a brilliant, fab-o idea, let's tell Mom and Dad.

ALEXIS

And, besides, you can't walk into Mr. Chow's looking like that.

Alexis waves her thin, pointy chin in Lulu's direction.

LULU

What's wrong with the way I look? I think my outfit looks cool. California surf style, right?

ALEXIS

Wrong.

LULU

Lex, this is about having inside information. You know Mom loves getting a scoop. She's so into knowing everything before anyone else.

ALEXIS

Most people do! I do. Don't you? OK, fine. And BTW, NOT chic on the outfit front. You look more like a bad Dr. Seuss character.

ELANA

No more fighting. You girls wanna stop here or no?

LULU

Yes, por favor. And can I bring in the lemon bars left over from school today?

ELANA and ALEXIS

NO!

Elana pulls up to Mr. Chow's valet.

ELANA
(out the window to Petal)
Hola, Miss Petal! You wanna call Mr. or Mrs. Harrison and tell them that these two are on their way in to see them?

As soon as the valet opens her door, Lulu bounds of out the car like a frisky puppy.

CLOSE UP ON ALEXIS. Knowing that she will be entering one of the most deeply cool old restaurants in the whole city, she lingers in the car to apply lipstick, brush her hair, and pop in a breath mint. Her outfit is perfectly put together—J Brand skinny-leg black jeans hugging her ankles just above her sky-high-heeled black Marc Jacobs booties. On top she wears an off-white short-sleeved peplum shirt under a merlot covered blazer. Before leaving the car she makes sure her black PS1 cross-body bag angles perfectly across her narrow torso.

INT. MR. CHOW—CONTINUED

Mr. Chow is a sophisticated restaurant that attracts L.A.'s famous and fashionable. It's got THE über-stylish low-key vibe.

Lulu bounces past the hostess. She plunges into the restaurant, hunting for her parents. Alexis follows at a distance, glancing sideways at the diners, not wanting to be too close to her over-excited, wild-haired little sister.

Lulu spots her parents sitting with STAB, who has a wiry but solid body and thick, sandy blond hair. He wears narrow black pants and a black sweater. This guy's got inner cool that makes him ageless.

Lulu hurries to her parents' table.

> LULU
> Mom! Dad! I've got fantastico news! Have you started eating? Can I tell you? Remember we were talking about my birthday? Well, now Alexis is planning this massively hot party.

> ALEXIS
> (totally embarrassed by her sister's blathering)
> Hip. Hip party, Lulu.

Elana reaches the table, watching everything like a mother hen.

> ELANA
> Hi, Mr. and Mrs. Harrison. It's OK? The girls wanted to come by to say hi.

As usual, Lulu's father seems laid-back and playful.

> **LINC**
> Well, Elana, it's always great to see you, but I don't know about these two.

> **FIONA**
> Elana, Alexis, Lulu, I'd like to introduce you to our friend Stab. He's in town for a couple of days recording a track for my new movie.

Elana immediately sticks out her hand.

> **ELANA**
> Con mucho gusto!

> **STAB**
> (responds in British-accented Spanish)
> Con mucho gusto!

Alexis tries mightily to play it cool. She's meeting one of the world's biggest rock stars! She's totally unprepared. During her moment's hesitation, Lulu jumps in.

> **LULU**
> Hi, Mr. Stab! Nice to meet you. I was just coming to see my parents about my birthday coming up in less than thirty days. I'm mucho excited to tell them about it, because for my birthday last year, they were in Africa.
> (to her parents)
> Remember, you guys couldn't come?

LINC
(to Stab)
Lulu is my amazing child who can speak forever without a break.

FIONA
(to the girls and Elana)
Actually, last year Stab came by my *Silver Water* set outside Johannesburg.
(now to Stab)
That was an unforgettable week. I still can't believe that I just shut down filming and we all took off. The studio went insane on me.
(back to girls and Elana)
Stab has raised millions of dollars for African children living in poverty. Linc and I traveled with him to a village in Tanzania. It was amazing to see what Stab brought to this village: schoolbooks, running water, and a nurse to immunize children.

Alexis is beyond starstruck. She cannot speak or move in Stab's presence. Lulu, on the hand, cannot keep still.

LULU
Stab, how many children live there? And what kinds of food do they eat? Like, can they grow crops? How do they get water? It must be hard to grow crops there! I'd like to go there and help grow food because—

LINC
(smiling, he interrupts Lulu)
See what I mean? Lulu's mouth doesn't need to take in
air while motoring along.

STAB
(eyes zeroing in on Lulu)
Lulu, your Mom and Dad are going to let me take you with
me next time I go. Pinky swear you'll come?

Stab and his accent are magically charming. Lulu stretches out
her finger. Stab crooks his around hers.

ELANA
We're leaving now. The car is with the valet, and I told
him we'd only be uno minuto. Good night. Buenos noches!

Knowing instinctively that the girls' moment with their parents
and the famous friend is over, Elana shepherds Lulu and Alexis
from the table and out of the restaurant.

EXT. MR. CHOW'S VALET—CONTINUOUS

Lulu and Alexis scramble into the car.

LULU
Alexis, you never told them about the party! I thought
you were gonna explain everything.

ALEXIS
(practically screaming)
Who could say anything over your nonstop yakking?!

Alexis boils. She missed an opportunity to impress Stab, and now she heaps her anger onto Lulu.

SCENE 7: WHO'S IN, WHO'S OUT?

INT. BEVERLY HILLS HOTEL COFFEE SHOP— SATURDAY, LUNCHTIME

This pink and green old-fashioned coffee shop is a hub of activity. Twenty-five stools line the long, curved counter where Alexis and Lulu sit. A rectangular mirrored case with glass doors holds delicious-looking pies, cakes, and Jell-O cups.

Lulu stares at the offerings. EUCARIO, the long-time waiter behind the counter, knows everyone—except, of course, the tourists.

ALEXIS
(to Lulu)
Now, I went through your school directory. I've got a guest list on my computer, but basically, it's most of the girls in your grade, plus Linc and Fiona's friends' daughters. Just girls. Let's keep it simple.

LULU

There's nothing simple about the girls at my school.
They, ummmm, don't like me. They never talk to me
except to ask me to explain science or math homework.

ALEXIS

Trust me, they'll all want to come to the Bel-Air retreat
of super-hot Linc Harrison and Hollywood power woman
Fiona Harrison for a très fab party.

LULU

Yeah, but it's MY birthday party, not Mom's or Dad's.

ALEXIS

You'll be Tween Queen for a day. You'll love it! The wanna-
be-cool-fifth-grade-girl brigade will love it.

LULU

What about Mom and Dad? They'll love it?

Alexis pretends to study the menu. There's a long pause. Lulu
draws in her breath.

LULU

Who else's on the list? My friends, right?

EUCARIO

Hi, Lulu. Hi, Lex. Are you ready?

LULU

Hi, Eucario. May I have my usual, please?

ALEXIS
Garden salad. Dressing on the side. Water, no ice.

Eucario winks at Lulu and moves along. It's a bustling lunch hour.

ALEXIS
About whatever you ordered—

LULU
(cuts in)
Oh, I know you're gonna make fun of it being a drippy
sandwich, but it's not. It's a turkey burger with cheese
and Russian dressing. And I'll eat it neatly! I even
brought my own chips and salsa.

Lulu reaches into her canvas tote bag that reads "Save Earth. It's
the Only Planet with Chocolate." In a swift, practiced move,
Lulu pulls out a chip and crunches it in her mouth.

ALEXIS
Besides your lunch's ooze factor, you've got to cut out all
the cheese, meat, and cream. And stop always smelling
like you're wearing salsa–corn chip perfume.

Eucario slides a tall vanilla milkshake over to Lulu. Lulu unwraps
the straw and takes a strong suck.

LULU
Talking about food, Sophia wants to make my birthday
cake, and I don't—

ALEXIS

Rewind: back to guest list. Look, Lu, this might come as a total shocker, but Sophia is NOT at this party.

LULU

What?

Eucario brings their food.

LULU
(slides away her plate)
I don't think I'm hungry anymore. Alexis, she's my massively mucho supreme best friend!

ALEXIS

There's a mission here. Super deluxe, très fab spa party. It's gonna have a certain vibe. It's not the kind of party where you can sit in a corner and hang out with just ONE guest.

LULU

Geez peas! She's come to every party I've ever had. How can I not invite my best friend who once when I was really sad made me laugh so hard milk sprayed out of my nose?! And she's even been to the emergency room with me and Momny, twice! Once when I cut myself with an apple corer, and once when I fell out of our kumquat tree.

ALEXIS

Plan a private party with her up in your attic playroom. I'm outta that one.

With that, Alexis looks up to see her boyfriend, ROBBIE, arrive with a group of boys and take a seat at the opposite end of the curved counter. Alexis walks over to them. Robbie waves at Lulu. Lulu waves back.

Enter Pop Girls. They appear in miniskirts paired with cropped sweaters. They circle the small coffee shop, pushing past Lulu.

                          LULU
                 (brightly but with effort)
    Hi, guys! Are you, ummm, having lunch too? I love the
    food here, but I, ummm, bring my own chips and salsa.

                          JANA
    We can smell that.

The Pop Girls give each other looks like they just stepped into a geek hole and don't want to get stuck in it.

                          LULU
    Hey, I'm gonna have a birthday party in a few weeks and...

                          JADE
                        (bored)
    Superb. I'm sure we'll all read about it.

Confused, Lulu feels her face getting hotter by the minute.

                          JANA
    Hey, FYI, red doesn't really match orange.

LULU
I'm not. I mean, I'm only wearing orange.

JANA
Are too. Your face. Way RED!

JADE
Check the text: you're always wearing orange. Like it's Halloween!

Pop Girls snicker. Alexis swoops back to her empty stool. She immediately understands what's going on. One thing about Alexis: she's got super-sonic girl radar.

ALEXIS
Oh, Jade, Jana, Jenna.

Pop Girls snap to attention. They're a little freaked because Alexis knows their names. Alexis represents the supreme cool teen girl ideal.

JADE
Hi, Alexis, ahhhh—
(nervous giggle)
Harrison.

ALEXIS
FYI: I'm doing ultra-fab party planning. It's a spa bash. My 411 tells me that no one in your grade has done one yet. So, I'll help you all glam up in honor of Lulu's b-day.

JADE
(friendly to Alexis)
Cool. Doing e-vites?
(unfriendly to Lulu)
Lulu, I'm surprised you're not having a mad scientist party!

Jana and Jenna cackle at their friend's wisecrack.

LULU
(ignoring the put-down, or maybe not noticing it)
Ya know, I really like experimenting, but I also spend lots of time doing other stuff, like cooking and gardening—

Alexis does a major cut-in and puts the smackdown on Jade.

ALEXIS
We're going for something classier than e-vites on this one. You wouldn't know this, but our parents, Linc and Fiona, go for distinctive, chic paper invites. You'll be schooled in the concept when it arrives.

Without thinking, Lulu reaches into her Save Earth tote bag and snacks on a chip dunked in salsa. The scent of fried chip and salsa cuts through the cramped space where the girls are bunched together. A glob of salsa plops onto Lulu's orange skirt. Pop Girls follow the drop with their eyes, roll them, then move away.

Jenna slows and looks back at Lulu.

JENNA
Hey, I went to a spa in Palm Springs once and loved it.

Jenna hurries to catch her pals.

ALEXIS
(hissing quietly to Lulu)
What did I tell you about eating?! It's like our conversations never happen!

LULU
I didn't mean to.

ALEXIS
Whatever. Let's go figure out invitations.

Alexis eats a few forkfuls of salad. She stands and leaves money on the counter. Then, she shakes back her hair, winks and waves good-bye to Robbie, and exits the coffee shop. Lulu takes quick, giant bites of her lunch, wraps what's left in a pink linen napkin, and drops it in her tote bag. She trots out to catch Alexis.

SCENE 8: THE PLEASURE OF YOUR COMPANY IS REQUESTED

INT. SUGAR PAPER—AN HOUR LATER

Sugar Paper neatly displays sophisticated letterpress-printed stationery. The tiny store is bright and clean. The stylish owner,

CHELSEA, is slim and wears fitted white jeans, a gray shirt, and an elegantly draped blue scarf.

Lulu bursts in.

> **LULU**
> (to Chelsea)
> Does your store really do letterpress? 'Cause I do flower pressing. And I've pressed more than flowers, like leaves and little bugs. Well, the bugs were already dead. Once I even pressed fifty blades of grass. My friend Sophia and I did it, but it was really hard to keep the grass from blowing off—

Alexis cuts in sharply.

> **ALEXIS**
> Hi, I'm Alexis Harrison. I made an appointment.

> **CHELSEA**
> Of course. Are you ready to get started?

> **ALEXIS**
> I need fifty invitations for a spa party. It's going to be totally fabulous, so the invitation has to reflect the party's très perfect awesomeness.

> **CHELSEA**
> I understand. Have you chosen a color scheme?

While Alexis and Chelsea discuss invitations, Lulu snoops around.

She opens boxes of stationery. She pulls greeting cards out of their slots. Nothing she touches ends up in its original place—cards go back upside-down, in the wrong slot, or in different boxes.

Chelsea watches Lulu from the corner of her blue eyes. She knows the Harrisons are celebrity customers, but she's not pleased to watch her precisely organized store get shuffled into a mess.

CHELSEA

This would be a custom order? Sugar Paper believes in a stylish, personalized approach.

ALEXIS

Exactly. Your store does our holiday cards. Oh, and this year Fiona sent totally simple, beautiful Valentine's Day cards you guys designed.

LULU

I didn't know Mom did a Valentine's Day card.

ALEXIS

Before you pout up a storm because you didn't get one, remember that you got a Valentine's present from Fiona.

LULU

Yeah, but it was the SAME Tiffany floating heart necklace I got from her last year.

Alexis studies stationery samples.

> ALEXIS

OK, I love the polka-dot envelope liners.

> CHELSEA

Let's begin with paper options then move to layout, typefaces, and lastly, color and liners.

> LULU

Hang on! Lex, how long can this take? I already know what they should say.

Lulu fishes through her tote bag till she finds a crumpled orange paper. She hands it to Alexis.

Alexis shoves it back into Lulu's bag.

> ALEXIS

Not happening. There're rules and proper ways to write invitations.

> CHELSEA

I apologize, but what's the occasion for this spa party?

> LULU

It's my birthday, and it WAS my party.

Lulu's throat tightens. She's not sure if she wants to yell or cry. Lulu feels Queen Bee taking over. It's not for nothing that she and Sophia have been calling Alexis "Queen Bee" ever since they could talk.

ALEXIS
Lulu, CHILL! And, hello?! STOP messing up the store.

Chelsea nods slightly.

LULU
(calmer)
You couldn't sneeze in this store without messing it up.

ALEXIS
If I'm doing this party, I need ABSOLUTE control.

LULU
Geez peas! Fine, but no matter what party you invent, I
want it ON my real birthday, February 26. It's a Sunday.
I checked.

ALEXIS
It's one possible date I've considered. But can you just
control you inner babyish self for a moment? A hip party
like this takes thought and planning. I'm throwing a
party your parents will want to go to.

At the mention of her parents, Lulu stares at Alexis with interest.

ALEXIS
I've gotta focus on the guests and what they'll like
and dislike.

Elana squeezes into the small store.

ELANA

Hola, ladies. Making invitations?

LULU

Haven't even started.

ELANA

Well, Lulu, when you're done, the Garzas' truck is outside. Miguel is asking for you.

 CUT-A-ROO! I LOVE Señor Garza and Miguel! Miguel's already thirteen. We met playing at the park when we were babies. His dad was working on his taco truck, parked nearby. Mr. Garza didn't have money to open a restaurant, but he's a *fantastico* chef. Mr. Garza's truck has been rolling around L.A. long before all these new fancy food trucks started showing up. Back to: ACTION!!

LULU

Perfecto! I could really use a tamale!

ALEXIS

You dropped salsa and Russian dressing all over your skirt at lunch. Is there any room left for tamale plops?

Meanwhile, Chelsea reorganizes everything Lulu mussed and moved. She has no idea who the Garzas are, but she thinks it's a great idea for Lulu to go see them.

LULU
(to Elana)
I don't want to watch the *Alexis Orders Invitations* reality show.

ALEXIS
Don't you think Lulu should be here to pick invitations?

ELANA
(no-nonsense tone)
Since she was one years old, Lulu could speak. So, Lulu, speak! What you want?

LULU
Here's what I want: I want whatever paper kills the fewest trees. It can take a hundred years to replace a mature tree. Do you have paper made from bamboo? That's the fastest-growing tree. Also, whatever colored ink should be from plants. Native American girls, like my age, made ink from berries and roots. We shouldn't have to use chemicals either.

ALEXIS
(cuts in)
OK, little Junior Ranger Brownie Girl Scout. You just got yourself excused from ordering invitations.

Chelsea has no idea how to handle the situation. She's used to relaxed calm. Elana, however, does.

ELANA

I told you girls, I need to pick up a yoga mat for your
mother then get her unsweetened vanilla almond milk.
I'm busy. So, here's how it goes: Lulu, leave now and say
hola to Garzas. Alexis, you got twenty minutos to make
invitations for the fiesta.

Elana's even-but-firm speech ends the bickering. Lulu practically skips out of Sugar Paper.

Alexis mouths "sorry" to Chelsea.

SCENE 9: HOLY GUACAMOLE!

EXT. SIDEWALK AT THE CORNER OF 26th STREET AND BRENTWOOD TERRACE—CONTINUOUS

A bright white food truck with the words "Taco Truck Numero
Uno" painted in red and green on both sides is parked on a side
street. Written in small black letters next to the service window
is "Señor Pedro Garza." A big white A, the city health and safety
inspection grade, hangs nearby.

MR. GARZA and MIGUEL stand inside the truck waiting for
customers. They wear clean white aprons that say "The Taco
Truck" and L.A. Dodgers baseball hats. Mr. Garza's thick silver
hair and Miguel's shiny black hair stick out of the sides.

Miguel leans out over the truck's service area as soon as he spots
Lulu coming down the street. He waves.

LULU
(shouts)
Hola! One tamale, por favor!!

MR. GARZA
Pronto! Coming right up for my numero uno customer.

Miguel leaps from the driver's side door. He and Lulu high-five.

MIGUEL
I wanted to see you today.

LULU
I'm having a shopping day with Alexis.

MIGUEL
Really?

LULU
It's a long, kooky story. The pronto version is it's my
birthday soon, and I want my parents to come.

MIGUEL
Sounds pretty normal to me.

LULU
No, wait. Ya see, Alexis has to plan a party mucho
fantastico so they'll come.

MIGUEL
I don't comprende that one, Lu.

MR. GARZA
(calling from inside truck)
Almost ready, Lulu!

MIGUEL
Quick, Lulu, I gotta tell you a secret.

Lulu stares wide-eyed at Miguel. She's never heard him use a serious tone like this before. He's always been a silly joker who's made her crack up since they both guzzled apple juice from sippy cups.

MIGUEL
(almost in a whisper)
Business hasn't been too good. Dad might have to shut down the truck and—

LULU
WHAT?

MIGUEL
—find another job.

MR. GARZA
(yelling)
One tamale! Hot and fresh.

LULU
(to Mr. Garza)
Gracias! Your tamale's my most ever perfect favorite food.

(to Miguel)
And do what?

MIGUEL
Don't know. Maybe just try to work as a cook somewhere?

Elana approaches the truck, greets Mr. Garza, and takes Lulu's tamale.

ELANA
(calling out)
What's with the whispering? Hola and adios, Miguel.

LULU
Momny, did you pay for my tamale?

Elana looks puzzled but reaches into her purse and pulls out five dollars. She hands it to Mr. Garza.

MR. GARZA
You loca, Lulu! Your money's not accepted here! Go. Adios!

Elana takes back the money. Then, she leads Lulu, clutching her hot tamale, toward the car.

SCENE 10: THE ACADEMY AWARDS!

INT. HARRISON KITCHEN AND EATING AREA— MONDAY, BREAKFAST

It's me, LULU. Scripts aren't really supposed to do this, but, again: CUT!! I've got to tell you something important: food. It's what gives us life and energy. And, well, this whole idea of never eating anything yummy is nutty. I live in a family of food freaks.

My mom and sister don't even like food. I secretly believe that my dad does, but he goes along with this food-isn't-good thing. Mom and Alexis eat in a way called vegan that, I think, means eating what vegetarian birds would eat. Seems like vegans only consume beans, rice, and small hills of salad—never anything from an animal. I like fruits and veggies, especially from my garden or the farmers markets. But I also LOVE red meat, cheesy anything, and my absolute favorite food, as you know, is Mexican.

Besides our chef, Michelangelo, who cooks dinner, and Elana, who prepares breakfast and lunch, I'm the only other person who uses our kitchen. Mom and Dad are way too busy making movies to make food. So, welcome to my family meals. Back to: ROLL 'EM!!

The girls are out of school. It's a "grading day" for teachers so the Harrisons have a rare morning together in their gigantic kitchen. The counters are covered in Italian white marble. The floor is dark wood. Steel appliances gleam. Copper pots hang from the ceiling.

Lulu mixes pancake batter while Elana watches to make sure Lulu gets the lumps out. Watson, wearing a yellow shirt that says "SECURITY," circles Lulu with his tongue hanging out, hoping to catch batter droplets like a child trying to catch snow-flakes. Linc, Fiona, and Alexis sit around a long wood table.

Linc reads a new script on his iPad. Alexis and Fiona discuss the best places for hairstyling and manicures.

> ALEXIS
>
> Here's what's on my list for the party: hair, nails, facials, and massage.

> FIONA
>
> Call the Bel-Air Hotel. They could send a whole crew, and they're so close to the house, their spa staff could practically jog here.

> ALEXIS
>
> What about using all your regular stylists and, well, I can't imagine not having Eve do the massages.

> FIONA
>
> Even though Eve is Lulu's friend's mother, she's not coming to do massages at a girl's birthday party. She's got the clientele A-list. Even I have trouble booking her on weekends.

Lulu monitors Alexis's conversation.

> LULU
> (to Alexis and Fiona)
> Hey, guys, Eve will come if Sophia's at the party.

> LINC
> (focused on his iPad)
> What's the date, babe?

LULU

It's on my real birthday, right, Lex? Isn't that what's on the invitation? The whole party's gonna be relaxing. Ya know, time to take deep breaths and get your hair polished.

ALEXIS
(to Lulu)

It's get your hair "done" and your nails "polished."

FIONA

Alexis, contact my assistant, Lilac, to get your call put through at the Bel-Air Hotel spa. So who's coming to this posh bash?

LULU
(jumping eagerly into the conversation)

It's called Spa-tacular. I made up that name. That's the only part Alexis let me do. My other job, though, is making sure you and Dad are Number One on the guest list. The other people, I don't know. Alexis, who is coming?

ALEXIS

Ummmm, well, I invited the Ditts' daughter, Jupiter, and Pamela Nicklesun and girls from Lulu's school. The guest list's just right. I'm starting to get into the food. I'd like to stick with spa cuisine but, you know...
(rolls her big, violet eyes)
...Lulu is bugging me for more food than that.

FIONA

Lex, I'm going to stop you there. All good ideas, but I have to get my face put together and my clothes on. I'm visiting shooting locations today.

Fiona gets up from the table, leaving a half-eaten fruit plate and a disappointed Alexis.

Suddenly, a cell phone symphony blares. The house telephone rings, adding another layer of sound. No one knows what to answer first. Fiona and Linc simultaneously reach into pockets and pull out iPhones. Elana answers the kitchen telephone. There's a moment of silence. Ringing, buzzing, chiming, and music all stop. The answerers listen.

FIONA
(unemotional, into phone)

OK.

Fiona's face turns into a stony mask. She clicks off her call with a sharp jab of her fingernail.

ELANA
(excitedly)

Dios mio, gracias!

Linc tosses his phone into the air. It somersaults twice. Linc catches it. Then he pumps his fist in the air.

LINC

YES!

Lulu dashes to the table.

LULU and ALEXIS

WHAT? WHAT HAPPENED?

Linc leaps from his chair and wraps his arms around both daughters.

LINC
(slowly, drawn out)

Well, that was Steve, my loyal and devoted agent. He called to inform me that I, Lincoln Grant Harrison, the son of simple, poor, but hardworking Oklahoma migrants, have been...

(excitedly)

...nominated for an Academy Award for Best Actor!

Lulu and Alexis whoop. Elana does a little shriek. Fiona remains still as frozen pudding.

LULU

For *Silver Water*? That's mom's movie!

LINC

Which was nominated for Best Picture!

FIONA
(flat and clearly unhappy)

It's not exactly MY movie if it was only nominated for Best Picture.

Fiona doesn't show a sliver of happiness. She's about to exit the kitchen.

LINC
(scowling towards his wife)
Can't you cut thinking of yourself even for a moment to just congratulate me?! This is my FIRST nomination for Best Actor. It's a big deal for me. YOU directed me brilliantly.

FIONA
(groaning)
Oh, please.

LINC
You've already won an Oscar for Best Director. See that Picasso I bought you after you won?
(points toward a drawing hanging on the wall)
I'm sorry you didn't get a Best Director nomination for the hundredth time!

Linc and Fiona fight as if no one else is in the room. Finally, they realize that everyone is quiet and staring at them. They're embarrassed to quarrel in front of the children and Elana. Fiona marches toward the kitchen door.

FIONA
(punching her phone screen)
Lincoln, I'm going to need a meeting with you in my office. ASAP. I'll head there right after I dress. Lilac will get agents, managers, and publicists all there too. We'll also have to meet with the studio.

(barking orders into her iPhone)
Lilac! First thing—cancel all my location visits for today!

Fiona exits the kitchen. An awkward pause lingers for several seconds.

LINC
Fiona wants me to report for work. After that news? I was thinking we'd go to Disneyland!

LULU
Oh, Daddy, I'd love to go to Disneyland with you. If you can't go today, can we go another day? Geez peas, we could do that for my birthday! Maybe Sophia could come too? Kids get to do that, ya know. Invite a friend and go to Disneyland for their birthday.

LINC
Do they still have Tom Sawyer's Island? I'd hide out there till Disneyland Security would find me—

The intercom buzzes. Elana picks up the receiver.

ELANA
(into receiver)
Yes, he still down here.
(pause)
Yes, Mrs. Harrison, I tell him.

All turn to face Elana, who obviously was just given instructions.

64

ELANA
(to Linc)
Mrs. Harrison wants you and your agent, Steve, to know plans have to be made muy rapido. The Academy Awards is in three weeks, so...

She trails off, embarrassed at having to deliver this message.

Lulu's face turns serious. She calculates numbers in her head.

Linc turns his joking manner on especially high so that Elana doesn't feel uncomfortable about having to deliver his wife's stern message and to smooth over the bitterness in the air.

LINC
I am summoned to war, ladies!

Alexis and Elana giggle.

LINCOLN
I take leave so that I may go into battle against other Hollywood male actors who shall viciously try to wrench this Oscar from my grasp! Off I go...

Linc kisses Alexis and Lulu on the cheek. He salutes Elana and exits the kitchen.

SCENE 12: NOT A GREAT DATE

INT. HARRISON KITCHEN—MOMENTS LATER

Uneaten food remains on plates strewn about the large table. Linc's iPad lies next to his fork. It's like someone pushed a gigantic PAUSE button on the morning's activity.

> LULU
> (frantic)
> When are the Academy Awards? Momny, do you know?

> ELANA
> I don't know, Lulu. Your mother just said soon.

> LULU
> When you were telling Dad, you said three weeks.

> ELANA
> Yes, your mother said like that, "three weeks."

> LULU
> That's when my birthday is! But what day?

Alexis switches on the kitchen computer and Googles "Academy Awards."

ALEXIS

Well, Lulu, you're gonna have to get over this one, but the Academy Awards are on February 26.

Lulu's green eyes immediately sting.

LULU

My birthday Spa-tacular isn't sounding too good right now.

ELANA

What, niña, Lulu? Don't cry.

LULU
(through tears)
Why does my birthday have to be on the EXACT same day as the Academy Awards?! And my parents, of all the girls in the world's parents, are in it! I'm massively happy they got nominated, but my deepest birthday wish was to have my family together.

ALEXIS
(almost warmth in her voice)
That's why I need to make this party so über-fab that they'll just HAVE to come. Leave it to me, Lu. I'll work my magic. This is Hollywood, right? Happy endings are us!

LULU
(perks up at Alexis's unexpected kindness)
Thanks, Lex, but Mom and Dad are gonna be too busy. I'll be forgotten again.

ALEXIS

Don't feel sorry for yourself. And use a tissue! Your nose
is dripping all over the kitchen.

Alexis stands up from the table then sniffs and freezes.

ALEXIS

It smells like raw sewage.

LULU
(tears streaming down her cheeks)
Oh, Watson probably ate too much batter. He'll be OK.

ALEXIS

Too bad about that.

Both girls look over at Watson, who's lying on his back, four
paws in the air, and tooting wind through his pull-up diaper
that inflates with each puff. Lulu cracks a smile.

ALEXIS

Now cut the waterworks.

Alexis pauses just before the kitchen door.

ALEXIS

I'm going to my room and don't want to be bugged. I've
got serious planning to do.

Alexis exits. She's clearly on a mission.

LULU
(turning to Elana)
Momny, you and Sophia are the only ones who understand me. All I wanted was a party with my family and best friend. Now Queen Bee has taken over.

ELANA
Niña, your sister is trying to help.

LULU
And, most worst of all, my mom and dad won't come.

Tears flow down Lulu's face again.

ELANA
Lu, give your sister a chance to help you with the fiesta. Maybe you two find ways to get your parents to come, at least for part of it.

Lulu wipes tears and snot on her sleeve.

LULU
Do you think they'd do that? Come for some of it?

Lulu ceases crying. Her animated self slowly returns.

ELANA
Listen, here's what I tell you: don't give up hope so easy! You and Alexis try doing something together.

LULU

Me and Queen Bee? Sophia and I are sure she has ten stingers. One under each of her shiny, polished nails.

ELANA

That's not the way to feel about your sister.

LULU

But she makes me feel freaky geeky. Like I don't even belong in this family.

ELANA

No, niña, my love. Nobody make you feel anything on the inside except you! You the boss of how you feel.

Lulu is quiet while she swirls her fingers in the pancake batter.

LULU

OK, maybe I'll go for it. I mean for once, really trust my sister. Maybe believe...
(sighs)
...in her.

ELANA

She says she wants to make your dream come true.

LULU

Well, here's to Queen Be—
(stops herself)
I mean...to Sister Power!

Lulu sticks two fingers into the pancake batter and licks them clean. She leans over and tightly hugs Elana, who isn't bothered by Lulu's batter-and saliva-coated fingers.

 CUT!! See what I mean about my Momny, Elana? She's like Mary Poppins, if Mary Poppins blew in from Mexico and lived in a place where she didn't need an umbrella. Back to: ACTION!!

ACT II: BIRTHDAY PARTY UNPLUGGED

SCENE 1: LET'S MAKE A DEAL

INT. BRIGHT BLUE PRIUS—SATURDAY MORNING OF THE FOLLOWING WEEK

Elana drives through thick L.A. traffic. Lulu slouches in back. Alexis sits up front.

> ALEXIS
> Elana, why's there SO much traffic?

> ELANA
> The traffico? Always the same. Never changes.

> LULU
> (to Alexis)
> Hey, talk about changing, I bet you think I'm gonna beg you to adios the Spa-tacular. Well, just the opposite! Let's go for this party! Make it fantabulous. That's the only way Mom and Dad might come. Lex...

Lulu pauses because she's about to say something she's never said to Alexis before.

> LULU
>
> ...you're right.

Alexis twists her whole body around to look at Lulu. Lulu expects a tender or surprised reaction.

> ALEXIS
>
> Of course I'm right! Look, I wouldn't get involved with a party if I didn't want it to turn out très perfect. MY name and reputation are on this one.

> LULU
>
> And Mom and Dad will wanna come to a party that's, ummm, cool, right?

> ALEXIS
>
> It's gonna be über-cool, no matter what! Lulu, I've already sent the invitations. And BTW, you can't call fifty girls and say, "Sorry, I'm not having my party anymore because Mommy and Daddy aren't coming to it." On Planet L.A., that's not only rude, it's social suicide!

> LULU
>
> The Awards are at night, right? My party's during the day. SO, Mom and Dad could come?! Maybe for some of it.

> ALEXIS
>
> That's called a "stop by," and that might work.

LULU

You've gotta ask them! I'm betting one hundred percent that you'll pull off the coolest birthday that any girl in LA LA Land has ever had. The only itty-bitty *poquito* request is that you get Mom and Dad there.

ALEXIS

When it's the right time, I'll call Lilac and...what's Linc's new assistant's name?

ELANA

Leif.

ALEXIS

Right. I'll chat up Lilac and Leif and get some 411. And, BTW, bet one thousand percent on me pulling off the best party ever.

LULU

I'm in for two thousand squared!

ALEXIS

Drop the brainy, whizzy stuff. If I'm gonna make you the reigning b-day princess, you've gotta get with the program.

LULU
(with more confidence than she feels)
Deal!

CUT!! Can you believe that my parents are best reached through their assistants? Lilac and Leif decide when and where my parents go and who they talk to. That's so unfair to me, their kid! Back To: ACTION!!

SCENE 2: A BLOW OUT

All day Lulu tags along with Alexis as she whizzes through party shopping and planning. There was Joan's on Third food store (where Alexis ordered tofu skewers, dried berry couscous, and grilled asparagus for the party); Bellacures nail salon (Lex selected nail polish colors); and Balloon Celebrations (Alexis examined every style, size, color, and shape of balloon).

Alexis and Lulu now sit in stylist chairs at Dry Bar, a hair salon that ONLY washes and blows dry hair.

ALEXIS
(to Lulu)
Blow outs totally have to be offered at the party.

Alexis's long hair is just about done. It lies down her back like black silk. Lulu's hair is another story.

LULU
Lex, let's get outta here when your hair's done. I gotta get home and see Sophia. This is taking way too long.

ALEXIS
That's YOUR fault.

> ### LULU
> NO it's not. I'm sitting still, even though this blow dryer blasts my scalp and neck with burning air.

Alexis stands. Her hair is done.

> ### ALEXIS
> It's your fault because you never brush your hair. It took fifteen minutes just to get your hair combed out.

The STYLIST spins Lulu's chair around so that she sees herself in the mirror. Only the hair on her left side is blown straight. The other side hangs limp and wet.

> ### LULU
> I don't even like my hair all flat.

> ### ALEXIS
> You will when it's done.

Alexis walks up front to pay. With Alexis not looking, Lulu gets up.

> ### LULU
> (to stylist)
> I'm done. Thanks. I, ummm, I like curly hair.

Lulu walks over to Alexis, who's twisting and angling herself so she can see the back of her hair. She holds out her iPhone to Lulu.

ALEXIS

Lu, take a picture of the back of my hair.

LULU

I don't know how exactly.

Alexis puts her phone on camera and instructs Lulu how to point and push the screen. Lulu pushes a few times, and Alexis grabs back her phone to look at the photos.

LULU

Now let's go.

ALEXIS

Are you kidding? Right now you look like a reject from a Muppets casting call.

SCENE 3: WORKING OUT THE DETAILS

INT. BRIGHT BLUE PRIUS—FIFTEEN MINUTES LATER

Elana drives Lulu and Alexis through Bel-Air's giant gates, past perfectly mowed grass, carefully shaped bushes, and huge houses.

Wearing headphones, Alexis listens to music while checking her Facebook page.

Lulu taps Alexis's shoulder.

LULU

Are you mad at me?

ALEXIS
(sliding headphones off one ear)
Here's how it works with A-1 Hollywood party planners, stylists, and decorators. You get a few precious hours of their time, and they focus their mega talents on you. You drop everything to be available.

LULU

I'm totally in. Geez peas! It's just that I didn't know today was a WHOLE day of party shopping. Next time you book me for a Saturday, I'll just tell Sophia I'm busy.

ALEXIS
(turns to look at Lulu)
You'd tell Sophia that you're too busy for a playdate because you gotta get ready for your birthday bash she's not invited to?

LULU
(trying to not get frustrated)
Not exactly gonna say that, Lex, because she's gotta be invited! Sophia's mom works all day on Saturdays so it's always our play day. We harvest the salsa garden. We bake. Or sew. We just, ummmm...draw and make up games and stories—

> ALEXIS

Fine. Then invent a story about why she can't attend your très fab party.

Stung by Alexis, Lulu is quiet a moment and looks out the window. She wonders how to make Alexis understand that NOT having Sophia is NOT an option.

> LULU

Saying Sophia can't come is like saying you have to spend a day without your iPhone. She's part of me!

> ALEXIS

Puhleese! Drama queen.

Alexis plugs herself back into her iPhone and slides her headphones back over both ears.

Elana expertly zooms the Prius through the Harrison gates, passing Sophia's mother, EVE, exiting the grounds in her yellow Mini Cooper. Eve rolls down her window and waves. Her earth-toned gypsy blouse billows around her arm. Eve is a Japanese woman in her midthirties and naturally beautiful. Her tightly braided hair swings over her shoulders as she turns her head and backs down the driveway.

SCENE 4: NOT THE USUAL PLAY DATE

INT. HARRISON HOME—CONTINUOUS

CUT!! Here's what you should know about going in and out of my house: you're always putting shoes on and taking shoes off. Street shoes inside might scuff up the floors or get dirt specks on the precious antique carpets. My house is cleaner than any hospital. It's dust free, bug free, and dirt free. Built-in humidifiers and air purifiers hum all the time. Fiona hates sneezes. If she can get rid of the dust in the house, she can control how much sneezing is going on. So, you can understand why I spend lots of time outside. Now, back to: ACTION!!

Without taking off her shoes, Lulu bursts through the tall, front doors into the high-ceilinged entrance hall. Dark, polished wood floors look like the surface of a pond at night. A crystal chandelier glimmers high above a sweeping staircase.

Shoeless, Sophia sits on the edge of the bottom stair. She reads a book called *Good Bugs*. Two jars sit next to her.

LULU

(panting)

Hey, Soph.

Looking up from her book, Sophia seems as if she needs to remember where she is. She looks very small, huddled on the stairs in the grand room.

SOPHIA

Hi, Lu.

Lulu nabs a chip from her tote and munches. An awkward

silence settles between the girls. Lulu's sure this is the first time that's ever happened.

> SOPHIA
> (tentatively)
> I brought them.

Sophia glances at the jars sitting next to her.

> SOPHIA
> Looks like they're slowing down. Probably getting hungry. They need to be let free.

> LULU
> Ummm...what? Oh, you brought them. Great.

Lulu covers up forgetting what Sophia was supposed to bring. Her head spins with Alexis's demand that Sophia not be part of the Spa-tacular.

Sophia picks up one of the glass jars beside her.

> SOPHIA
> The ladybugs came in the mail yesterday. Perfect timing so we can release them on the roses today. They're so cute, but they're losing their buzz.

POW!! The great day they'd planned slams back into Lulu's memory. When *she* was in charge of her party, Lulu planned to mix up a batch of rose perfume as her party favor. When she and Sophia went to collect the petals, they found tiny bugs munching up the rosebushes. Ugh, that all seems like another lifetime!

LULU
(now excited)
Geez peas! Let's get outta here and bring the ladies to their new home.

Lulu grabs both jars and dashes out the front door. Sophia follows, pulling on her shoes before heading outside.

EXT. HARRISION ESTATE ROSE GARDEN—CONTINUOUS

LULU
What else did *Good Bugs* say? If I remember, the ratio was: ten ladybugs cover twenty feet, so if we need to cover an area of a hundred feet, we gotta release fifty bugs. That's what you ordered, right?

SOPHIA
Exactly. You worked out the math last week.

LULU
We need these ladybugs to be mucho hungry to eat the aphids. Hernandez said aphids are what's destroying the rosebushes. Look, they're eating everything except the thorns.

The girls inspect the tattered plants.

SOPHIA
We could also release spiders. They eat aphids too. And they won't harm the roses since they're carnivores.

LULU
Yah, but can you imagine my mother knowing I was releasing spiders near her house?

The girls giggle.

SOPHIA
Your dad wouldn't be bothered.

LULU
You're right. He'd probably threaten to let them out in Mom's bathroom just to see her freak out. Then he'd laugh about it, so she'd get madder...

Thinking about the bitterness between her parents, Lulu loses her giggly-ness. Lulu and Sophia sprinkle water and gently toss ladybugs onto the rosebushes.

SOPHIA
You know, Lu, you're lucky to have a mother and a father. Even if they fight. My mother's worst day of the year...
(pause)
...is Father's Day. She feels so s'bad—remember, we made that up for sad and bad?

LULU
'Course I do.

SOPHIA

Well, my mom feels so s'bad that I don't know my father.
And I can tell she's lonely. She'd love to have someone to
tease her about spiders.

LULU

Sophia, you're really brave. I'm a wimp.

SOPHIA

Nah. I just don't know anything different.

LULU

Well, that just shows what a weakling I am, because my
parents have been fighting my whole life, and I'm still
not used to it.

How could Lulu explain to Sophia that when her dad teases her
mom there's a sharp bite to it? Like it's meant to draw blood.
How can she explain that her mom is so busy and demanding
that she doubts her mom has ever hugged her dad? Sensing
Lulu's distress, Sophia changes the subject.

SOPHIA

So now that our ladybug army is on the attack, let's go
check the cilantro plants. Your garden-grown salsa is
gonna be the hit of your birthday party, Lu.

As if this day could get worse! Between dealing with Alexis and
the Spa-tacular and worrying about Sophia, Lulu's done, wiped.
Her stomach starts its nervous swirling.

LULU

Soph, I've gotta lie down.

Lulu drops the watering can she'd been holding and sinks onto the thick, freshly cut, Technicolor-green grass.

For a moment, Sophia is puzzled. Then Sophia falls to the ground next to her friend.

TIGHT SHOT ON THE GIRLS as they rest on their backs watching the bright blue sky. Not a cloud to be seen.

LULU

There's nothing in the sky except sunlight and ultraviolet light that we can't see with our naked eyes.

SOPHIA

I remember when Mr. Ling taught us that last year. You were SO excited to learn about rainbows!

LULU

How 'bout we lie here until ten things, anythings, fly or float in the sky above us.

SOPHIA

Ok. There's a scrub jay.

LULU

Oh, there's a golden-crowned sparrow.

SOPHIA

Two!

LULU

Remember when we used to count fairy clues?

SOPHIA

Yeah. We'd hunt around the garden looking for signs that fairies lived here.

LULU

And when we found eight clues, we were convinced they were here because a sideways eight looks like fairy wings.

The girls lie on their sides, tracing their fingers through soft grass, lost in the world of fairy figure eights. WATSON shuffles up and licks their faces. They giggle.

A tall, lean man, JOHNNY WALKER, leans over and scoops up puggy. He's wearing purple corduroy pants and a blue satin blazer. Johnny adores dressing up, even though he deals with Watson all day.

 CUT!! Really super quick. I wanna tell you that Watson's manny, Johnny, is SO amazing. He ALWAYS seems to know what's going on. He understands dogs AND people perfectly. And he can handle any situation. He plays with, cooks for, cleans up after, and exercises Watson, plus he does anything for the family that Elana needs help doing. Back to: ACTION!!

JOHNNY
(voice is playful, like he's suppressing a laugh.)
Oooh, I love when Watson makes his surprise slurp attack! C'mon, Dream Team, stop lollying around and do something useful. Let's go shopping! Watson needs his summer wardrobe.

Lulu and Sophia pull each other up. They follow Johnny and a waddling Watson to Johnny's Canine Cruiser, an old Cadillac painted red with silver magnetic paws slapped on the trunk and hood.

The girls dive into the back seat with Watson. Johnny puts on his red driving cap. The girls smile. An afternoon with Johnny Walker is just what the doctor ordered!

SCENE 5: A LESSON IN BEING TOP DOG

INT. CHATEAU MARMUTT—LATER THAT AFTERNOON

Lulu, Sophia, Alexis, and Johnny Walker with Watson strapped onto him in a baby sling walk into Chateau Marmutt. Alexis had to be picked up at Robbie's house. She almost fainted from embarrassment when the canine cruiser pulled up.

Chateau Marmutt looks like a mini-castle, with chandeliers and a back wall painted with country scenery. It's a place a dog can be treated royally.

Chateau Marmutt offers dog aromatherapy, grooming, haircuts, brush outs, fresh-breath treatment, and nail cutting.

Lulu picks up a flier advertising "Marmutt Spa's Private Parties." Lulu files that idea away for Watson's next birthday. If she's doing a spa party, so should puggy!

Dog clothes hang or are neatly folded around the store. Lulu sorts through doggie shirts stacked under a sign that boasts the clothing is "eco-friendly, zero waste, locally made."

SOPHIA
(shyly)
Does Watson need summer clothes? It's never really cold.

JOHNNY
It's got nothing to do with COLD, darling Sophia. It has everything to do with COOL! Alexis, don't you think so?

Alexis glances up from her iPad.

ALEXIS
Johnny, you could make any furry-legged creature win an Oscar for Best Dressed.

JOHNNY
(responding quickly and brightly)
You're right-o. And it doesn't need to be furry. If Wilbur was ever up for Best Actor in *Charlotte's Web*, I'd do wonders for that little piggy!

Johnny holds up a black cashmere sweater with matching beanie.

JOHNNY

Just look at this number!

Lulu and Sophia crack up, not only because of the idea of a pig in a swanky sweater, but because of the way Johnny poses while holding the pieces.

ALEXIS

Ya know, this shopping spree reminds me, Lulu. You should find something Watson can wear to your chi-chi party.

Sophia shoots Lulu a confused look. Johnny jumps in and covers for Lulu, whose face has clouded with worry.

JOHNNY

Oh, puhleeeeese! If Watson ever attends a VIP party, I'm making his outfit. And, of course, I'll be coming in a matching one!

Sophia remains silent and pretends to study the bakery display filled with doggie doughnuts and hand-painted cookies shaped like squirrels and fire hydrants.

LULU

Soph, why DON'T we make Watson's clothes? You're awesome with a needle and thread.

SOPHIA
(quietly)
I don't think I could finish clothes for Watson in time for your party.

LULU
Oh, forget my birthday. I meant to wear anytime.

ALEXIS
(to Lulu)
Speaking of your birthday, we've gotta ramp up party clothes shopping.

JOHNNY
Excuuuuuse moi. This shopping excursion is about Watson. OK, how cutie-pie are these?

Johnny holds up two dog outfits, a black T-shirt that says "FEED ME" in rhinestones and a red sweater. THE CASHIER rings them up.

JOHNNY
Next, we have to stop for some organic beef, ground especially for Watson's raw diet. The smell in that place! Putrid!!

ALEXIS
You can drop me and Lu to shop at Fred Segal. Sophia, you can come.

LULU

I'd rather watch Watson's beef get ground.

SOPHIA

Me too.

SCENE 6: THE RULE OF SCHOOL

INT. CROSSWINDS SCHOOL CAFETERIA—MONDAY LUNCH

 CUT!! You're gonna think I'm super strange after I tell you this: I'm the opposite of every other fifth grader because *I like classes more than recess and lunch*! Recess is when the Pop Girls troll around like a pack of hyenas, giggling at anyone who crosses their path. Lunch is when you're judged by where your fanny lands. If you sit with goof-offs, you're considered a troublemaker. If you sit with sports lovers, you're a jock. Of course, the Pop Girls table is by invitation ONLY.

None of this bothers me and Sophia because we're meant to be together. Our second grade teacher called us "shoes and laces." When Sophia and I go to the cafeteria, no one saves us spots. We always find each other and sit wherever there's room. Back to: ACTION!!

CAMERA PANS TO FOLLOW Lulu as she wanders around the Crosswinds cafeteria, looking for Sophia.

JANA

Hey, Lulu!

Lulu, unsure Jana really means to call *her*, walks slowly to the Pop Girls' table.

LULU
(caught off guard)
Oh, hi, Jana. Hi, guys.

Lulu glances around the Pop Girl table, AKA, Pop Girl Island.

JADE

Party info, puhleese.

                    JENNA

Yeah...so spa day, cool. You're doing facials, right?
What else?

                    JANA

Mani-pedis?

Jana rolls her eyes toward Jade after spotting Lulu's unpolished,
uneven nails.

                    JANA

Well, maybe not.

                    LULU

Oh sure, there'll be all that. Alexis, ya know, my sister, is
arranging everything.

Pop Girls exchange interested looks. Noticing this, Lulu plunges
onward, though she's also scanning the lunchroom for Sophia.

                    LULU

Yeah, Lex is my party-planning professional.

                    JADE

What hair stuff? I'm supposed to have my hair
straightened this weekend, but if you're having a full
salon, I'll wait. Who's the stylist?

Having made eye contact with Sophia, Lulu now wants to join
her friend. She also wants this conversation over because she
doesn't have answers.

                    LULU
Oh, sure, ummmm, yeah, we're doing hair.

                    JENNA
More than braiding with beads?

                    JADE
Hey, we did that for my fifth birthday party. Remember
that one? We had the henna tattoo lady, and Jana wanted
a henna tattoo on her bum?!

Pop Girls snicker. Jana giggles the loudest, trying to hide her
obvious embarrassment at the memory.

                    LULU
Well, I hope you guys can come.
                  (pauses)
See ya, gonna have lunch now.

                    JADE
You can eat here. Jana, move over.
             (Jana scootches but isn't pleased)
Hey, what's the chow at the fête?

                    LULU
Well, Lex has that covered too. Third, ummm, not Third
Street Promenade...something on Third.

Lulu makes no move to sit down.

JENNA

You mean Joan's on Third?

LULU

Right! All that low-fat stuff. Hey, listen, talking about food, I'm pretty hungry and wanna get Sophia. Can we fit one more? Great!

Lulu doesn't wait for an answer. She leaves her "Go Green" lunchbox on Pop Girl Island and dashes off to get Sophia.

Lulu finds Sophia. There's an empty spot, clearly where Lulu is expected to sit. Not that anyone else would sit next to Sophia. She's known as the quiet, boring kid who's really smart in English.

LULU
(unsure)

I came to get you. Let's sit at Pop Girl Island today.

SOPHIA

Are you kidding?
(waving at the empty space)
We both have room here.

LULU

I know it's weird, but they invited us to sit there.

SOPHIA

Oh no they didn't. Maybe they asked you, but there's no way they said, "bring your geeky friend."

LULU
Soph, they didn't say THAT.

SOPHIA
Look, I understand why they want you. It's OK.

Suddenly, Lulu is sure Sophia knows about the Spa-tacular. She should have invited her already! Panic smacks her! Red bursts through her freckled face. How'd it slip out? Her stomach flips so many times she thinks she'll never be hungry again.

SOPHIA
It's not your fault, so don't feel s'bad.

Hearing Sophia use their secret, made up word makes Lulu feel very sad and bad.

LULU
It wasn't my fault, I mean—

SOPHIA
(understanding)
Just go sit with the Pop Girls today. I know they want to talk about your dad's Academy Award nomination. It's so exciting. It moves the Pop Girl's Cool Meter.

LULU
(panic passing)
Oh, I'm sure you're right!

SOPHIA

Yeah. I didn't think Jana waved you over to get your
frosted lemon squares recipe. Those girls are so skinny,
I'll bet they think lettuce with dressing is a dessert.

Lulu and Sophia laugh. Lulu is relieved.

LULU

OK, just this once.

Lulu turns to swim the turbulent social seas back to Pop
Girl Island.

FADE OUT.

SCENE 7: FAMILY STYLE

INT. HARRISON DINING ROOM—WEDNESDAY EVENING

Once a week the Harrisons try to have dinner together. The
weekly dinner only happens when both parents are available on
the same night. Sometimes weeks go by without a family dinner.

Lulu, Alexis, Fiona, and Linc sit around a huge, oval, polished
wood table. It's set with sparkling silver and crystal. Linen
napkins rest on each person's lap. Elana directs A SERVER who
places food on each person's plate.

LULU

There's an essay contest at school, and the winner

represents Crosswinds at the California Global Warming conference. Can you guys help me? Ya know, just look over what I wrote?

Fiona moves a sparse fava bean salad around her plate.

FIONA

Lu, this is such a busy time of year. When is your essay due?

LULU

Next week. It's mostly done. Mom, you're such a leader saving the rainforests. Please read it! You'd love what I wrote!

FIONA

Email it, Lulu. Get it to Lilac and include the turnaround time.

LINC

I could read it too.

LULU

Geez peas, Dad! I'd love that! I did a section about how you went surfing in Mexico twenty years ago, and when you went back to surf the same spot last year, you said the water, reef, and marine life had changed.

LINC
(gives Lulu a wink)
I'm in your report? Crazy cool. That's the closest I've ever gotten to academic success.

FIONA
(to Linc)
OK, enough with the dumb hick idiot act! I've got too much riding on *Silver Water*. Have you been learning to answer reporters' questions so you sound confident?

Fiona grabs the iPhone resting next to her plate and checks calendars and schedules.

FIONA
(ignoring the girls)
Is your agent getting you ready for the Academy Awards? What about your hair? Lilac keeps asking me because she hasn't heard back from your assistant, what's his name?

LULU and ALEXIS
Leif!

LINC
(anger in his voice)
You could just ask me.

FIONA
(cold, sharp tone)
You cannot blow this one. Your nomination is not just about YOU.

LINC
I speak English, babe. You're saying my nomination is because YOU directed me! Told me how to talk, move, even breathe in each scene. So I better win.

FIONA
(anger seeping from each word)
That's crazy and totally unfair.

ALEXIS
(unmoved by her parents' warring words)
Being a stylist is my DREAM job.

LULU
(voice trails off)
I'd like to be a marine biologist. Or gardener. Or chef. Or, ahhhh...well, a secret thing...

LINC
(to Lulu)
Like a secret agent? A spy?

FIONA
(to Alexis)
You do NOT want to be a stylist. You hustle stores and designers for clothes, shoes, and jewelry. Then, the star you're dressing usually doesn't like what you bring them. So back you go to your designers and beg for another wardrobe, more shoes, and bigger jewels.

ALEXIS
(delighted to be engaging her mom)
I bet I'd get tons of free stuff from designers who'd want my actor or actress to wear their stuff.

LULU
(to her mother)
How long does it take? Like when do you have to start
getting ready for the Oscars?

FIONA
Dressing a star for one night can take weeks.

LULU
I mean, how long will it take you and Dad to get ready?

FIONA
(testy and impatient)
Well, Lulu, as you can tell, we're getting a trifle more
ready each day.

Alexis realizes that Lulu is zeroing in on the conflict between her
Spa-tacular and Academy Awards. She's seriously furious that
Lulu interrupted her conversation with Fiona.

Alexis shoots Lulu a look to BACK OFF.

The server clears plates while Elana enters holding a tray of mini
sundaes. Watson waddles behind, his nose raised high. He sniffs
loudly. Toddling in a dessert parade is his favorite exercise.

ELANA
Dessert?

LULU
I think Watson wants one.

Linc flashes Lulu a smile.

FIONA

No, thank you, Elana.

LULU

Mom, does that mean Watson can have two?

FIONA

I'm concluding dinner. Thanks, girls.

Fiona gets up from the table and glances at Linc, who's shoveling pudding into his mouth.

FIONA

Linc, for the next couple weeks, lay off the cream, butter, and egg foods.

Fiona exits.

ALEXIS

See, Lulu, I tell you the same thing.

Linc twirls his spoon toward Lulu, takes another bite, then abandons his dessert. Apparently, his appetite has faded.

SCENE 8: FASHION WORLD FOR THE UNFASHIONABLE

INT. FRED SEGAL—THURSDAY AFTER SCHOOL

CUT!! You gotta know how hard shopping is for me. Shopping takes time away from other things I'd rather be doing, like saving one redwood tree, one acre of rain forest, one sea turtle...even one taco truck. Besides, clothes should be (1) orange; (2) soft and cozy; (3) able to get muddy, buttery, or ripped; and (4) long enough to cover my pale, freckly skin. Back to: ACTION!!

Lulu and Alexis enter Fred Segal, a haven for trend-setting L.A. fashion. This L.A. style destination is made up of small, stylish boutiques all under one roof. Alexis strides directly into the children's shop.

Lulu slumps into a chair and pulls tortilla chips from her tote bag.

Alexis finds SERENA, the most warm, fun sales gal. Serena's sweet, natural charm draws Lulu right in. Alexis likes Serena's mid-back-length blond hair.

SERENA
(approaching Lulu)
It's your birthday soon?! Awesome. Try some dresses on so I can get a feel for what you like.

ALEXIS
(quietly to Serena)
Please, don't ask her what she likes. You'll be stuck hearing about her geeky ideas.

LULU
(to Serena)
OK, here's what I don't like: anything tight or short, and
positively nada with ruffles. I like clothes that cover my
arms and thighs. So NO micro-mini clothes. And orange,
please! I love orange.

ALEXIS
Whoa!!

LULU
(plunging on)
If possible, I'd like a skirt, and, of course, natural,
organic fabrics that don't use chemical dyes.

ALEXIS
Forget it! Just try on dresses.

Serena and Alexis pull dresses off racks.

Lulu ducks into a curtained changing area. Serena carefully
hands dresses in to Lulu.

After a few minutes, Alexis yanks open the red velvet curtain
to reveal Lulu, half-dressed. Lulu immediately FREAKS. She's
extremely shy about her newly developing body and desperately
tries to cover herself.

ALEXIS
(annoyed)
OMG—would you get over it! How can I possibly see the dresses when you're hiding in here?

LULU
I'll come out and show you! Go away!

Lulu drags the curtain closed.

LULU
(shouts from inside the dressing room)
These dresses are all too small. What size are they, a kids' 4?

ALEXIS
I can't imagine you need bigger sizes.

LULU
(frustrated)
If I try these dresses on, they might rip AND be mucho short.

SERENA
(gently)
Ya know, I'm gonna dash into one of the women's boutiques and see what I can find. Back in a sec.

Alexis stomps over to a nearby full-length mirror to examine her own outfit: tight moto jeggings with leather paneling on the sides paired with trendy leopard loafers and a sheer short-sleeved button-down that shows off her naturally tan, slender arms.

> **LULU**
> (still inside the changing room)
> Lex, I'm not like you. I have my own style, and I like how
> I look in my clothes!

Alexis doesn't respond. She adjusts the deep purple cashmere sweater tossed over her shoulders while squeezing her forest green clutch under her arm. She LOVES looking like she's between photo shoots!

Lulu sits on the dressing room floor feeling overwhelmed: big, bored, and hungry. Alexis doesn't believe in lunch stops.

Serena returns.

> **SERENA**
> (hands Lulu two dresses)
> Here, cutie. Try these. I think they'll feel better. They're
> from an awesome boutique next door.

A hanger clacks to the floor.

> **LULU**
> (relieved)
> Hey! These aren't so short. Thanks, Serena. I really like
> this sparkly one.

Alexis rips open the curtain to inspect the outfit.

> **ALEXIS**
> Not happening! Sequins are for evening only. Try on
> that one.

Alexis points to a silk and wool navy women's tunic. On Lulu it could fit like a dress.

Command given, Alexis turns on her heels. Lulu draws the curtain tight.

Lulu emerges from the changing room.

LULU

Geez peas! This dress fits and doesn't look bad. It's just, kinda, my arms stick out. Does it come in long sleeves?

ALEXIS

It's perfect! I SHOULD be a stylist. You don't want to look like Princess Geek. It's fashionable to wear dresses above the knee and to show a little arm. Don't you ever read *Teen Vogue*?

LULU
(fed up)

What about a scarf to cover my neck and shoulders? I feel naked without another layer.

SERENA

I saw the perfect one!

Serena dashes out to another boutique, grabs some limp fabric, and swoops back.

SERENA
(opening the scarf)

108

Ta-da! These two-toned scarves are from next door. The material's soft, and this navy and orange combination just pulls the outfit together.

Serena drapes the scarf around Lulu's neck.

> ALEXIS
> Oh, fabulous. I normally don't like orange, but this scarf rocks! Lulu actually looks fashionable. Well, except for those Vans.

> LULU
> What's wrong? They go great with this outfit.

> ALEXIS
> You're kidding, right? We'll go to Madison and get you some Lanvin ballet flats. Metallic. Goes with everything. They'll be the icing on the cake.

> LULU
> And speaking of cake, how 'bout we stop at Sweet Lady Jane down the street?

> ALEXIS
> Not even.

SCENE 9: TRASH IT

INT. CROSSWINDS SCHOOL—BEFORE SCHOOL

Lulu, Sophia, and other members of the Cleanup Club wander the hallways picking up candy wrappers, crumpled papers, broken pencils, and even uneaten food. They pitch everything into see-though plastic trashbags that say "THROW ME OUT." Mr. Ling, the club advisor, walks up.

MR. LING
I am continually confused by students throwing garbage on the ground when trash cans stand a few feet away.

LULU
It's not just kids, Mr. Ling. When I do beach cleanups, there's tons of garbage thrown away by grownups too.

MR. LING
I stand corrected. Litterbugs come in all sizes. How is your next beach cleanup project coming?

Kids pass by on way to their lockers. They mutter, "gross" or "barfy."

SOPHIA
Lu, I think kids don't like these bags.

Sophia raises her bag and shakes the mess inside.

LULU
(wide smile spreads across her face)
Well, I ordered these clear bags just so people CAN get grossed out by seeing what washes onto the beaches.

MR. LING

That's clever as long as those who throw the trash come
to help pick it up.

The Pop Girls, dressed alike in black leggings and sleeveless
blouses, come down the hall and stop to open their lockers.
They sniff and then fake gag.

LULU

Hi, guys. I'm organizing a big beach cleanup, so we're
trying out these cool bags.

JADE

Just looking at those bags rates way high on the totes
disgusting meter.

JANA

And going to the beach to get smelly trash sounds worse
than going to the beach in the rain.

LULU

But it's easy and important to pick up trash. Any plastic
wrapper or bottle can be swept up by wind or the tide
and carried into the ocean or a lake or stream. Ya know,
all places trash shouldn't be.

JENNA
(to Jade and Jana)

Don't you guys think it's kinda funny that the bag says
"THROW ME OUT"?

JADE and JANA

NO!

JENNA

Yeah, I guess. But I once saw a story about this island of trash floating in the middle of the Pacific Ocean. That was gross.

LULU

You're right! It's hundreds of miles wide and mostly made of plastic.

Jade slams her locker.

JADE

Now that I think about it, you're right, Lulu. Stinky garbage is way bad. How 'bout we all come over and plan the cleanup?

MR. LING
(looking at Jade, Jana, and Jenna)
Well, judging from your recent test grades, you could all use extra credit.

JADE

K. We're in.

Lulu hesitates. Are the Pop Girls really asking her for plans?

LULU

Geez peas. Great. I always need more help.

JADE

Will text ya what day.

LULU

Sure. Anytime. My momny, I mean my, ummm, Elana picks me up every day. She can bring you guys over.

Jade and Jana scurry down the hall. Jenna, seeing instant worry flash across Lulu's face, lingers.

JENNA

Do you not want us to come over?

LULU

No, it's just that, I'm not really a texter.

JENNA

Ohhh. OK, I'll just call your house when they figure out the day.

Jenna bolts down the hall to find her pals. Lulu looks at Sophia and shrugs.

LULU

That was muy loco.

FADE OUT.

SCENE 10: PUTTING THE "SPA" in SPA-TACULAR

INT. BEL-AIR HOTEL—SATURDAY, MORNING

CAMERA PANS TO FOLLOW LULU AND ALEXIS as they enter the Bel-Air Hotel.

They walk a winding path over a bridge, past fountains, then through courtyards full of azaleas and impatiens. Alexis pauses to check out sunbathers lounging around the huge pool. Lulu pauses to read room service menus hanging from hotel room doors.

The Spa, tucked inside the hotel's hillside European-style building, sits above stone steps.

The girls enter. Lulu lies down on a bench.

> LULU
>
> Geez peas! I've just walked miles on empty. Lex, you gotta believe in lunch breaks.

Lulu quickly looks around the spa's reception area and notices dispensers filled with fruit-infused icy water.

> ALEXIS
>
> Stop complaining already!

Alexis approaches the front desk.

LULU
If it wasn't for my chips and salsa, I'd lift the lid off that glass water cooler, plunge my hand through the ice, and snatch the apple slices. I'd risk first-degree frostbite!

Lulu grabs chips from her Save Earth tote and crunches.

The spa's director is a French woman named JOSETTE who glides over. She greets Lulu and Alexis with a kiss on each cheek (the European way). Josette wears fitted white trousers, a white silk blouse, and pointy high heels. Her hair is swept up into a bun. The French are always so stylish!! Alexis likes *everything* about Josette. Lulu wonders if Josette might have a good crêpe recipe.

JOSETTE
Bonjour, Harrisons. Welcome! We are a full-service spa for ladies and gentlemen to relax, refresh, and beautify.

ALEXIS
Sounds très fab! It's my sister's birthday, and I'm planning her party at our house.

Alexis shakes her small wrist, weighed down with a pile of gold bracelets, in the direction of the house. Her bangles clank against her large flashy watch that's never set to the right time.

ALEXIS
I wanted to see if you'd do the party.

JOSETTE

Oh, oui. I can create a highly personalized spa experience.
Of course, I just adore your parents!
(totally ignoring Lulu)
Alexis, please tell them that Bel-Air Spa is at their service.

LULU

Gracias, Josette.
(concerned voice)
Hey, Lex, about our parents. Have you checked if
they're coming?

ALEXIS

Just CHILL. This will be a way-perfect bash.
(to Josette)
So, can we pick treatments for tweeny girls?

JOSETTE

Oui.

Josette hands Alexis the spa menu and a gold pen.

Lulu checks her watch.

LULU

How long are we gonna be here? I don't want to be late
for Sophia again.

ALEXIS

If you'd use a cell phone, you could call, text, or email her.
What do you guys use, smoke signals? Sundials?

Josette interrupts. Bickering does not suit the spa's peaceful mood.

> JOSETTE
>
> Lulu, mon cherie, please tell me what treatments you'd like? Massage? We have caviar, Swedish, deep tissue, stone, aromatherapy, reflexology.

> LULU
>
> What? Caviar? People slather stinky fish eggs all over their skin?

> JOSETTE
> (smiling)
> No, it's not actual fish eggs. The creams we use have rare beads that only resemble caviar eggs.

> ALEXIS
>
> What about facials?

> JOSETTE
>
> Of course, there's a facial with white caviar. I also offer caviar manicures and pedicures.

Josette points out the facial and massage options on the spa menu.

> ALEXIS
>
> Do you have the staff for this?

> JOSETTE
>
> For the Harrisons, I do whatever it takes. I recommend

reflexology as the massage, so the girls don't have to get completely undressed.

LULU
I positively do NOT want to take my clothes off!

JOSETTE
I'm sure Alexis figures something out.

Alexis beams at the compliment.

JOSETTE
What about hair? All girls like to get their hair done.

ALEXIS
Well, judging from Lulu's locks, not ALL girls.

They turn toward Lulu, who's now exploring a mirrored, closet-sized room filled with lotions and potions. Lulu sniffs and squeezes every tube.

LULU
(yells out)
Are these organic? I hope nothing's tested on animals.

ALEXIS
(embarrassed by Lulu)
SHHH! News flash: you're in a quiet, relaxing place!

Lulu walks toward the spa's entrance.

LULU
I'm gonna wait in front for Elana to take me home.

Lulu pushes open the doors.

JOSETTE
(calling after Lulu)
Not to worry. Everything will be taken care of!

LULU
(stops and calls back to Josette)
Bonjour, bon voyage.

SCENE 11: FRIENDSHIP FLUBBED

INT. HARRISON HOUSE—FIFTEEN MINUTES LATER

LULU'S POINT OF VIEW as she jogs through the grand front entrance, up the winding mahogany wood stairs, and down a long hallway lined with silver-framed black-and-white photographs of relatives. She shoves open the door to her room, puffing and sweating, then collapses across the foot of her bed.

Lulu's room is the only part of the house that looks different. Walls are painted orange. Lulu somehow convinced her mother they'd look perfect colored like a Hermès bag. Bursting bookcases line the walls. Ivy garland winds up the posts of a canopy bed that's covered with a ladybug-embroidered duvet. Butterfly shaped pillows rest against the headboard. Watson, wearing his new "FEED ME" shirt, lies on Lulu's pillows doing his best impression of a stuffed animal.

French message boards decorate the walls, onto which Lulu has stuck drawings, postcards, animal pictures, and any kind of paper souvenir. Lulu herself ordered the orange furry beanbag chair and the wood sign on the ceiling that reads, "DREAM."

Sophia sits on the floor, knees pulled up to her chest. She's clearly made an effort to make herself as small as possible. She's reading a book called *Birds, Bees, and Buds: A Native Garden.*

> LULU
> (panting)
> Hi, Soph! I didn't forget. Today's our day to plant the wildflower seeds. You brought them, right? They came?

> SOPHIA
> Yes.

Sophia pulls seed packets from her fawn-colored Coach messenger bag, a Christmas present from Lulu's mother. She tosses the seeds onto the floor.

> SOPHIA
> They came. But I'm going.

A deep silence spreads through Lulu's bright, sunny room. Then, despite feeling wiped out from her zoom up to her room, Lulu clicks into action. Her emotions and energy explode.

LULU

I know I'm late. Alexis wanted me to do stuff again today. You know how she is: Queen Bee.

Sophia doesn't respond.

LULU

She's getting more into me lately, well, into my birthday. She's been taking me out 'cause she's trying to get me to be more grown-up.

SOPHIA
(mock surprise)

Really, more grown-up?

LULU

Exactly! Today I spent an hour in the glam-a-roo Bel-Air spa learning that a caviar facial doesn't slather fish eggs on your face.

More silence.

Sophia chews on the ends of her hair.

LULU

And being with Alexis is hard on my stomach. She doesn't let me have lunch. The only food in that spa was apple slices floating in icy water dispensers. I was so hungry I considered plunging my hand into the glass cooler, snatching out the apples, and risking the first-degree frostbite.

Sophia sits motionless.

Like air let out of a beachball, Lulu deflates.

More silence.

> **SOPHIA**
> I'm happy for you. You've always wanted to be close to your sister.
> (pauses)
> Don't think I don't understand. I wish I had a brother or sister to hang out with.

> **LULU**
> Soph! You know we're like real sisters.

Lulu rushes over and tries to hug her friend, but Sophia shrinks into an even smaller ball, hoping to roll out of sight.

> **SOPHIA**
> (in a sad, quiet voice)
> I just wish you'd told me.

> **LULU**
> I thought I told you I was going with Alexis this morning.

> **SOPHIA**
> No, not about that. I mean tell me, you know. Everything.

Sophia's eyes sweep across shopping bags strewn around Lulu's room. The bags are stuffed with clothes, shoes, and makeup. Lulu realizes what Sophia sees.

LULU

Oh, been doing some shopping with Alexis. She's decided I need a full chick-over.

SOPHIA

A what?

Lulu leaps over to a shopping bag and dumps out tubes of lotions and moisturizers.

LULU

A chick-over. Look at this crazy stuff. One of these tubes has stuff I'm supposed to use to cover my freckles! Like I'd ever want to do that!

SOPHIA

You mean chic-over?

LULU

Yeah, 'cause it's not like she'd ever help me harvest cilantro or make lemon squares.

An intercom buzzes. Elana's voice comes through.

ELANA

Sophia, your mother is *aqui*—waiting for you in the driveway. She say to come now, but that you're gonna have to wait for her at her next appointment.

Sophia unfolds herself and rises from the floor.

SOPHIA

Gracias, Elana. I'll be right there.
(looking at Lulu)
Since you're obviously really busy, let me save you the time. I'm leaving because friends can be different, but what they've gotta have in common is telling each other the truth.

LULU

(trying to keep her voice even)
Fine, well I can honestly and truthfully say you're making a grande mistake. Why do you want to sit around some stranger's house while your mom's doing a massage when we can be planting our seeds?

Sophia heads to the door.

LULU

(follows Sophia)
I'll come down with you and explain to your mom.

SOPHIA

(looks at Lulu)
No, thanks.

LULU

Soph, c'mon! You're my supremely best friend! We've got tons of recipes to make up and plants to grow and bugs and birds to watch and stories to—

SOPHIA

OK, Lulu.

(in the hallway, turns to face Lulu)
Ya know, your dad shouldn't be the only one up for a Best Actor award. You're pretty good, yourself.

Sophia leaves Lulu standing in her bedroom stunned.

 CUT!! Geez peas! I am SO confused! A Saturday afternoon, and I'm not with Sophia?! I don't know whether to sit, stand, lie down, go downstairs or outside. Well, I can't be a statue, so back to: ACTION!!

Lulu picks up the wildflower seed packets from the floor, flings them onto her desk, and slumps into her puffy desk chair. That's when her eyes see it.

Her creamy, raspberry-inked, letter-pressed Spa-tacular birthday invitation is tucked under a ribbon on the message board.

Lulu crawls into her bed and curls up next to Watson, who hasn't moved a millimeter.

LULU

(to Watson)
Thanks for all your help!

FADE OUT on Watson's sleepy face.

SCENE 12: HARD
TO STOMACH

INT. BLUE PRIUS—AN HOUR LATER

> LULU

STOP!!

> ELANA

There's traffic. Uno momento!

> LULU
> (her arm out the window)

It's Miguel! See him standing on the corner?!

Elana expertly turns right and goes around the block. She pulls up behind the Garzas' Taco Truck. Lulu's out of the car in a flash and bolts over to Miguel.

EXT. CORNER OF KINGS ROAD AND BEVERLY BOULEVARD—CONTINUOUS

> LULU

Geez peas, Miguel. I'm famished because I just lived through the most humiliating experience! Elana got me out of the house to shop with Alexis. And we're in this snooty towel store—well, they sell other snooty stuff too—and puggy jumps from his stroller and de-diapers! I dive after him under racks of expensive bathrobes. He's rolling in dust bunnies and colored strings. The more I reach for him, the more he rolls away from me. And all I can—

MIGUEL
(serious)
Lulu! We've got bigger problems than your crazy dog. Papa's for sure gonna have to sell the truck. Could be as soon as next month.

Lulu looks over at Señor Garza talking to Elana. There are NO other customers around.

LULU
How do you know?! That can't happen!

MIGUEL
Some guys came to the house the other night. Papa thinks I was asleep. He took them all through the truck. Showed them everything. How to grill, fry, and bake.

ALEXIS
(calling from open car window)
I've got to get home! Robbie date night! C'mon, Elana, please!!

LULU
You guys can't shut down the truck! There's gotta be an idea we haven't thought of yet.

ELANA
(calling out)
You want anything now, Lulu?

LULU
Oh, si! Elana, how 'bout we pick up dinner here for the whole family? We can get one of everything since we don't know what everyone would like.

ELANA
Yes we do. Nada. Your mother and sister not eating this food.

LULU
Right. OK, how about I bring it to school tomorrow? For all my, ummmm, friends. They've never tried it.

Alexis has gotten out of the car and walks over to Lulu and Elana to get them to hurry up.

ALEXIS
The so-called Pop Girls don't eat greasy Mexican food. Never have. Never will.

CUT!! I'm SO *mucho* boiling angry at Alexis right now. I feel like force-feeding her a beef tamale. I'm trying to save my pals' delicious business and total way of LIFE, and she reminds me that I'm surrounded by people who only eat kale. Back to: ACTION!!

LULU
Beef tamale, por favor, Señor Garza.

MR. GARZA
(big, warm voice)
Coming right up, Lulu.

MIGUEL
(whispering)
Lulu, ya know you can't order enough tamales to get us
out of this pickle!

Lulu stares at Miguel for a while. He pretends to be interested in
the uneven sidewalk he's kicking.

Mr. Garza hands Lulu a warm silver package.

MR. GARZA
Baked up hot and fresh!

Lulu takes the tamale and immediately unwraps and bites
into it.

LULU
(with mouth full)
Hey, Miguel, that's it: Bake sale! But, actually, I won't
sell the food. Let's see.
(pauses)
I'll bake something and put the Taco Truck name on it!

MIGUEL
Lulu, how you gonna write on food?

LULU
Leave it to me. I'm making a plan as I chew.

SCENE 13: THE SCHOOL SCENE

EXT. CROSSWINDS SCHOOL—MONDAY RECESS

Sophia acts polite to Lulu, but not like a friend, and definitely NOT a best friend. She barely answers Lulu's questions and doesn't start any conversations. Sophia skips recess to help Mrs. Tarvin, the English teacher, write analogy worksheets.

After Lulu gets over the s'bad shock of Sophia's changed attitude, she decides to hang out with the Pop Girls. Could turning eleven mean that life is moving in a different direction? Like new friends and even brushing her hair?

Kids run, catch, jump, cartwheel around a grassy field.

SLOW MOTION SHOT OF POP GIRLS ENTERING YARD AND ARRANGING THEMSELVES ON BENCHES IN THE SUN.

JADE
Ginormous shopping spree at Century City Mall! Check out these new bootie boots.

JANA

Totes ADORBS! Way wanted to go shopping all last weekend but slept at my dad's house in Malibu.

Lulu approaches. There's no room on the benches. She and her Save Earth tote plunk with a thud on the ground. She sits with her back facing the direct sunlight to keep the rays off her face.

LULU

Alexis took me shopping. We bought a dress for my birthday party. It's blue kinda-stretchy material.

JADE

That's soooo lucky that Alexis takes ya shopping.

LULU

You guys can all come next time she takes me.

JADE

Time and place?! We'll be there!

Lulu pulls out some tortilla chips and a small glass container of salsa.

LULU
(waves around the salsa container)
You wanna try it? Homemade and my secret recipe.

JENNA

K.

Jenna plucks a chip from the bag, dunks it in the salsa, and pushes it into her mouth.

> JANA
> (to Jenna)
>
> I hope you have mint gum!

> LULU
>
> I have an idea. Why don't you come early to my party so we can swim?

> JADE
>
> Maybe your dad will lifeguard?!

> LULU
>
> My dad used to be a lifeguard for Santa Monica beaches but that was when he was, like, twenty.

> JENNA
> (to Lulu)
>
> Swimming sounds fun.

> LULU
>
> And the pool's really warm.

> JENNA
> (to Jana and Jade)
>
> We could bring bathing suits?

LULU

Alexis wanted everyone to bring bathing suits anyway
to put on for massages or something.

JADE

Way too much to pack to bring over. I don't even know
what to wear to the party yet.

JENNA

Dresses?

JANA

Or skirts?

JADE

I think we should do skirts.
(tosses a look in Lulu's direction)
Prob NOT orange ones.

SCENE 14: HANGING (WAY) OUT

INT. HARRISONS' HOUSE—AFTER SCHOOL

Pop Girls wander around the huge kitchen and connected
"family" room. Lulu, excited to have her new friends over,
forgets to have them remove their shoes when they come in.
The Pop Girls' wedged and heeled shoes scuff the shiny floors,
but Elana, sensing Lulu's nervousness at having these girls over,
doesn't say a word.

JADE
(holding up a silver picture frame)
Do your parents really know Stab?

LULU
Is he in that picture with them?

JANA
Lulu, like you never noticed?!

LULU
Stab's really a great person. Do you know—

JADE
(dropping into a metal and leather director's chair)
Is this your mom's?

LULU
Ummm. I guess.

JANA
Whaddya mean, you guess? She's a director and this is a
mega-way-cool modern director's chair.

LULU
Yeah. She's a director. Let's go into the kitchen. Elana
and I put out my favorite food.

POP GIRLS TOGETHER
Chips and salsa!

The girls drift into the kitchen.

Fast as lightning, Jenna grabs a chip, dunks it in salsa, and crunches it in her mouth. Lulu smiles at her.

> LULU
>
> *Delicioso*, si?

> JADE
> (sniffing)
> Smells like Stan's Donuts in here.

> LULU
> I just fried cinnamon churros.

> JENNA
> You can make churros? Is it hard?

> LULU
> No, I just wear this hoodie jacket and put the hood up when I fry the dough so the oil doesn't splatter on me. That really stings.

> JANA
> The grease in here is gonna give me pimples.

> JENNA
> Churros are, like, my, I mean, my brother's favorite.

> LULU
> Hey! Maybe you guys can help me? My friend and his dad

have this food truck, called the Taco Truck. And, well, I'm trying to help them save it 'cause business hasn't been too good. So I started making cinnamon churros and putting them in brown bags that that have the name and phone number of the Taco Truck.

JANA

I thought a churro was, like, some kind of animal.

LULU

It's a Mexican doughnut, sorta, but without the hole.

JADE

I had a cart of them at my fifth birthday.

LULU

Well, I've been giving 'em away down at the Bel-Air East Gate around five o'clock.

JANA

Glad to hear you aren't eating them all yourself.

JADE

Barfy!

JENNA

You mean, you're doing all that just to help some dude?

JADE

Why even care about another monster chow truck chugging around?

136

LULU

'Cause Miguel, that's my friend, and his dad, Mr. Garza—the truck's their job. I mean, it's really their whole business.

JENNA

Did they ask you to do that?

LULU

Geez peas! I don't want them to know. I used allowance money to buy flour, sugar, oil, brown bags, and a stamper that says "The Taco Truck."

JADE

I don't have allowance money. I just have my dad's credit card number in my phone under his contact information.

LULU

Well, I don't have a cell phone, but I'd saved allowance money. The churros go pretty fast. It only takes about fifteen minutes of standing near Sunset to hand out forty free churros. So, if you guys'll help me, it would be even faster.

SILENCE.

Pop Girls drift back into the family room. Lulu follows.

LULU

Ya see, I want people to see the number on the churro bag and call to find out where the Garzas' truck is and go eat there.

                    JADE
I want to get myself sitting in your mom's chair on
Instagram.

Jade arranges herself in Fiona's director's chair and then tosses
her iPhone to Jenna.

                    JADE
    Take me!

Jenna puts the phone on camera and shoots. She gives it back to
Jade to post the photo on Instagram. Lulu looks on, confused.

                    JADE
I bet I get, like, a hundred "likes" from that.

                    JENNA
Hey, how 'bout we Instagram the churros and phone
number on the bag for your friend's food truck?

                    LULU
Whatever that is. If you think it'll help, I'm massively for it.

                    JANA
You know what Instagram is, right?

                    LULU
I'm guessing it's not a fast way to make graham crackers.

                    JADE
LULU?! You could be hopeless.

                    138

Jenna fills the awkward moment with a round of giggles.

> LULU

Wanna start planning for the beach cleanup? We can go up to my room.

> JADE

Let's go wherever your dad and mom usually hang out. I wanna chill out in their most fave place in the house.

> LULU
> (confused)

Ya know, I'm really not sure where that would be.

SCENE 15: MUNCH WITH A MESSAGE

EXT. JUST INSIDE BEL-AIR GATES—5:00 p.m.

Lulu's frizzy hair and burnt orange crocheted scarf flap in the breeze. She stands on a patch of grass next to the humongous white Bel-Air Gates, just before Sunset Boulevard. Johnny Walker lounges on a lawn chair he set up behind Lulu. He wears dark black sunglasses and studies a Hollywood stars map he bought on the corner of Carolwood and Sunset. Watson lies curled up on Johnny's stomach, also sporting dark sunglasses.

> LULU
> (yelling into the street)

Get your free churro and call the TACO TRUCK!

Lulu and her churro giveaway cause traffic to back up. Angry drivers in shiny cars honk.

> LULU
> Best Mexican feast on wheels!

A siren screams. A patrol car screeches to a halt alongside Lulu. It's Bel-Air Patrol, the private security company that protects the Bel-Air neighborhood. OFFICER GALE steps out.

> OFFICER GALE
> Hiya, Lulu!

> LULU
> Hi, Officer Gale. Want another churro today? Fried fresh!

> OFFICER GALE
> Mrs. Gale will kill me. Last night, I reported to her about the churro, and she couldn't believe I didn't save her any.

> LULU
> (hands over two bags)
> Here. Take one to her AND tell her to eat at my friend's truck.

> OFFICER GALE
> She'd love one.

> JOHNNY
> (calling out from his lounge chair)
> Any problem, Officer?

OFFICER GALE
(to Lulu)
Is Johnny supervising?

Lulu and Officer Gale look back at Johnny and Watson.

LULU
Yup. Johnny can't move, though, because Watson is asleep on him and any sudden jolt wakes puggy up.

OFFICER GALE
Lulu, I'm afraid this time I can't let a sleeping dog lie. I'm shutting down your operation.

LULU
What?

Cars continue to honk and drivers yell out, "c'mon" and "what do you think you're doing, kid?"

OFFICER GALE
Done with business here, darlin'. I'm getting too many complaints about the backup onto Sunset.

Johnny, cradling Watson in his arms, comes up next to the patrol car.

JOHNNY
Let me guess: my entrepreneurial Lulu doesn't have a business permit for this ritzy residential area?

LULU

But I'm not selling anything. I'm giving people free information about where to eat.

JOHNNY

Along with a delicious fried stick of dough!

OFFICER GALE

Lulu's slowing the traffic. Sorry. Not a good spot. Especially during rush hour.

LULU

What am I gonna do with all these leftover churros?

As Lulu lifts up a canvas tote bag filled with bagged churros, Watson wiggles awake as if his sweets-and-treats alarm went off.

JOHNNY

(jiggling Watson)

Well, the warm furry goodness in my arms can think of a few ways to get rid of 'em.

Officer Gale smiles and returns to his car but soon rolls down his window.

OFFICER GALE

Hey, Lulu! Mrs. Gale and I will be dining at your friends' Taco Truck ASAP. And tell them we're coming hungry!

SCENE 16: YOU'RE MELTING

INT. CROSSWINDS SCHOOL SCIENCE CLASS—AFTERNOON

Mr. Ling stands in front of the class.

> MR. LING
> My favorite class of the week. Kids Teach Today, K.T.T. Who'd like to start?

No one moves.

> MR. LING
> Anyone? Any interesting science topics on your minds?

Lulu squiggles and squirms. Sure. She's thought about one hundred zillion scientific things, but maybe being something of a Pop Girl, she shouldn't volunteer.

> MR. LING
> Lulu. Why don't you break the ice?

> LULU
> Ice? Hummmm. OK.

All eyes on her, Lulu slowly gets up from her desk and grabs a fistful of ice from the science lab's freezer and heads to the front of the room. If there's one thing that's certain, it's that she's not letting Mr. Ling down.

LULU

Anyone ever been to Lohachara?

SAM

The Chinese restaurant?

LULU

The Indian ISLAND. It's an island in the Bay of Bengal.
Or at least it used to be! It doesn't exist anymore. Ten
thousand people used to live on Lohachara but now
it's gone. It disappeared in 2006 and that makes it
THE numero uno inhabited island to be washed off
the earth.

The silence in the class is only broken by creaking seats while
bored students shift their weight. Meanwhile, Lulu continues
on while the ice she's holding melts into a puddle onto the floor.

LULU

The very first island to be washed underneath the ocean
was Kirbati. It was in the Pacific, but no one lived on it.
As oceans keep rising, bigger islands and whole chains
of islands are in serious danger, like the Maldives and
the Marshall Islands.

The class further zones out: doodling, whispering. Ignoring
Lulu. Without Sophia to keep her moving along, Lulu doesn't
know how to stop.

LULU

And not only tropical islands way out in the middle of

the ocean but really close islands near the United States could disappear too. Like Assateague! Did you guys read *Misty of Chincoteague*? That's one of our...
(looks at Sophia)
Ummmm, I mean, my favorite books. Assateague and Chincoteague are islands off the coast of Maryland or, ummm, Virginia where real-life wild ponies live. Those ponies could drown!

NO RESPONSE.

LULU

We can't let this happen, and we can all help. The ice I was holding all melted. There's a puddle on the ground that didn't used to be there. While the ice is kept cold, it doesn't melt, but because the atmosphere is heating up, glaciers and icebergs are melting and their melt is adding tons more water to the seas, and when the ocean rises—

MR. LING

Excuse me, Lulu. So much of this excellent information is in the essay you wrote for the California Global Warming Conference. I'm going to put a copy out in the classroom for anyone to read. Now, though, I'm going to ask if there's anyone else ready to teach.

LULU
(embarrassed)
Thanks, Mr. Ling.

Lulu, shuffling back to her desk, passes Sophia. Lulu keeps her head down but hears Sophia whisper.

SOPHIA
You should clean up your mess.

Sophia points toward the puddle of melted ice on the floor.

SCENE 17: STILL NO ANSWER

INT. HARRISONS' "FAMILY" ROOM—WEDNESDAY NIGHT

Lulu twists uncomfortably on the leather and metal director's chair. She reads a tattered copy of *Misty*. Her orange book light is clipped onto page 145.

A TELEPHONE RINGS.

ELANA
(over intercom)
Lulu, pick up line one, por favor.

Lulu reaches for a cordless telephone.

LULU
(hesitantly, unsure who would call her)
Ummmm. Hi, it's Lulu.

MIGUEL
(off screen)
Will you talk to my dad about painting the truck?

LULU
(relieved)
Oh, Miguel. Hi. Sure. Paint the Taco Truck? What do ya mean? It's always been plain white with the red and green writing.

MIGUEL
That's the problemo. All the newer trucks have totally cool paint jobs. They look like street art, ya know. Pictures. Cartoons. Graffiti.

LULU
Oh yeah. I've seen those around. They have really bright colors too.

MIGUEL
Exactly. So you gotta talk to my dad.

LULU
Why don't you?

MIGUEL
I did, but he won't consider it.

LULU
What'd he say? There's got to be a really good reason. Your dad's really smart AND a great chef.

MIGUEL

He won't say, but I think it's because of his mom.

LULU

Did she paint it or something?

MIGUEL

Exactly.

LULU

But I thought she—

MIGUEL

Yes. She painted it with my dad just before she died.

LULU

I get it.

MIGUEL

Hey, I loved *mi abuela* mucho, but this is business. Dad's gotta move on.

LULU

Nope. No way. There's meaning and magic in the truck because of your abuela, and it's gotta stay that way.

MIGUEL

But then the whole truck's gonna go! Be sold to someone who'll paint it over themselves.

LULU

Well, repainting the Taco Truck isn't the right answer.

MIGUEL

There's still NO answer. But, hey, I kinda knew you'd agree with my dad.

LULU
(seriously)
You got a great, *fantastico* dad.

MIGUEL

You got a great, *famoso* dad.

LULU

Yeah, but he sure can't make a tamale.
(draws a breath)
Miguel? Hasn't business picked up lately?

MIGUEL

Nope. Not really. Not enough.

LULU

Haven't had any more customers?

MIGUEL

A few new ones. But it's really weird. They've all tried to order churros.

LULU

Geez peas!

MIGUEL

Oh well. Bye, Lu.

 CUT!! Note to my readers: always CHECK the menu before you decide to hand out free stuff to advertise your friend's food truck! Make sure you offer something they actually sell. Back to: ACTION!!

SCENE 18: ROOM FOR IMPROVEMENT

INT. LULU'S BEDROOM—THURSDAY EVENING

Despite wearing super-tight, colored, skinny jeans, the Pop Girls lounge around Lulu's room. Jade sits on Lulu's bed with her back up against the pillows and her legs under the duvet. Jana lies at the foot of the bed. Jenna sprawls on the furry beanbag. Lulu, in her usual orange skirt and surf T-shirt, sits with her elbows propped on her desk and her head resting on her hands.

JADE
(working her iPhone screen)
Can you believe how many likes this girl got from a dumb photo of her hand with fake nails pasted on?

JANA

Lemme see.

Jana grabs Jade's phone, looks at the screen, and then passes it to Jenna.

JENNA

Well, she has each one painted a different color.

JADE

That's like a Sesame Street experiment.
(Turns on a mocking tone)
How many colors can you paint on five fingernails, kids?

LULU

May I see? I still don't get how the insta-pictures work.

JADE

Lulu, for someone so totally into science, you sure don't
know anything about modern technology.

LULU
(thinks a moment)
Ya know, that's right. I can learn, though.

JADE

How'd you get into science-y stuff anyway?

JENNA

Did you have one of those volcano erupting kits? I had,
ummm, I mean, my brother had one of those.

LULU

'Cause I tried an experiment that went grande wrong.
When we first got Watson, his poops smelled beyond
disgusting and gross. My mom got convinced there was
something wrong with him and wanted him gone. But he

151

was my Christmas present, and I begged her NOT to give him away. But, ummm, no one can really argue against my mom. So, the night before he was supposed to be given away, I decided to cure him of stinky-poop-itis.

JANA

Really? That's a disease?

LULU

Nah. But that's what I diagnosed.

JENNA

What'd you do?

LULU

OK, don't laugh. Remember, I was desperate.

JADE

Come on.

LULU

Well, I knew peppermint was supposed to make your breath fresh, right? So, Sophia and I gathered up all the peppermint we could find. We ended up with a shoebox overflowing with candy canes and peppermint sticks. Then, at night, I ground them all down and mixed it with leftover turkey and fed it to Watson.

JADE

That is HILLLLarious.

LULU

Now it kinda is. See, I thought the clean minty-ness would pass right through him and make his poop fresh.

JANA

Did it?

LULU

No. It almost killed him.

JENNA

How'd you save him?

LULU

I didn't. The vet did. And our dog manny, Johnny. Well, at the time Johnny worked for the vet and sat up with Watson all night long.

JANA

Well, you're way into dogs.

Jana rolls her eyes and tilts her head toward snapshots of dogs stuck onto a puffy French message board.

LULU

Oh, I wanna show you guys something.

Lulu reaches under her bed and slides out a mega-sized rectangular plastic bin filled with greeting cards. Each card pictures an adorable doggie. Lulu hands bunches of cards to each Pop Girl.

LULU

'Cause I almost killed my dog at Christmastime, I try to save other dogs. Johnny drives me to the pound, and I take pictures of dogs who need homes. We make the pictures into these holiday cards and send them to everyone, asking if they'd want a dog for Christmas.

JADE

Anyone EVER say yes?

LULU
(pointing to the wall)
Sure. All those pictures there are Christmas pooches.

JENNA
(glances over at Jade and Jana on the bed)
K. That does it. You guys, we've gotta show Lulu how to Instagram and group text. It'll be WAY easier for her to get people to eat tacos and rescue dogs.

JANA

Did you say "eat hotdogs and rescue tacos"?!

JADE

Lulu, do you even have an iPhone?

LULU
(softly)
Nope.

JADE

Any phone?

LULU
(even quieter)

Uh-uh.

JANA

Well, so much for that plan.

JENNA

I could show you on my iPhone.

Jenna pulls her iPhone covered in a purple sparkle case from her Burberry purse.

LULU
(still sitting on the floor surrounded by
mini-mountains of doggie holiday cards)

Really? It's, ummm, fine for me to learn on yours?

JADE

NO. It's NOT.
(to Jenna)

Put that away! Lulu could break it.

JENNA

iPhones are pretty hard to mess up.

JADE

Are you forgetting? I GAVE you that iPhone case.

Jenna stashes her phone back in her purse. Jade gets up and heads toward the door. Jana follows.

> JADE
>
> I heard a car. Could be my mom. Or maybe your parents? I wanna see who's here.

Jenna gets up, grabs her purse, and exits. Lulu, tripping over doggie Christmas cards, stumbles toward the door.

INT. ENTRANCE HALL—CONTINUOUS

Jenna sits a on a round mauve velvet bench and waits for her mom. The other Pop Girls have already gone.

Lulu plunks down beside Jenna.

> LULU
> (talking in her speedy way)
> Hey, maybe you can show me how to use your phone another time? Ya know, I can use it to tell people about important things.

 CUT!! This is a moment I've gotta break in on. Sorry, but look: I've NEVER had any interest in a cell phone before. I mean, I'm ONLY (almost) eleven! But, all of a sudden, what I do want is for the Pop Girls to be my friends, especially Jenna. It feels *mucho* important because she could teach me stuff that could help me be a better me! We could team up to rescue dogs or Mr. Garza's business or zillions of other people and animals and trees and plants and water that need saving. Now, back to: ACTION!!

Watson trudges sleepily out of the powder room, where he'd been napping.

> JENNA
> (looks at the pug)
> You have a cat too?

> LULU
> (laughing out loud)
> Geez peas, that's just Watson in his cat costume. Funny right?

> JENNA
> (now laughing)
> WAY weird.

> LULU
> Sophia and I sewed it. The hard part was the getting the whiskers to stay on. Look.

Lulu scoops up Watson and shows the brown elastic band that loops under the pug's ears.

Jenna bends in to see.

> JENNA
> Why'd you guys wanna dress him like a cat?

LULU

Puggy acts like a cat. He only wants to lie around all day and not be bothered. So, one day we decided we'd dress him like one.

JENNA

K. That's weird AND funny. So, I'm gonna put his picture up on Instagram. Watch.

Jenna pulls out her sparkly purple-cased iPhone, sets it to camera, and takes a picture of the puggy-kitty. She explains to Lulu how to post it. Immediately, likes ping into her phone. Everyone who follows Jenna's Instagram sees the picture of pug as cat and likes it.

Jenna and Lulu sit with their heads together and watch the responses come in.

JENNA

See! You could take a picture of your friend's food truck or whatever and, if you have a lot of followers, ya know, friends who also are on Instagram, they'd know about it.

LULU

Alexis showed me how to take a picture on her phone. I can do that!

JENNA

(looking at her phone, freezes)
Uh oh. Big thumbs down from Jade. Uh oh, megatime. I better wait outside for my ride.

Jenna stands and grabs her purse and phone. Lulu stands and picks up her pug as cat.

> LULU
>
> Can I ask you one really, mucho fast question?

Jenna leaps toward the front door.

> LULU
>
> Why do you have to do what the other Pop Girls do?

> JENNA
> (spins around to face Lulu)
>
> Because!
> (pause)
> Why do you always do everything with Sophia?

> LULU
>
> We do, I mean, did tons of stuff together, but no one was the boss. We were just friends and no one was in charge.

> JENNA
>
> News flash: I'm A POP GIRL! That's OUR way. They're MY friends!!

> LULU
> (softly—mostly to herself)
> But I'm your friend too.

LULU'S POINT OF VIEW AS SHE WATCHES JENNA run toward her mother's car pulling up the driveway.

SCENE 19: SWIMMING UPSTREAM

EXTERIOR—CROSSWINDS, FRIDAY LUNCH

> LULU

Hey, guys.

Lulu squeezes into a spot at the end of Pop Girl Island. The girls shift their bodies away from her.

> LULU

I met with Mr. Ling to show him the final plan for beach cleanup.

> JADE

Why waste time doing that?

LULU
(slightly confused)
Oh, I just, ummm. Well, he's interested in how many people are coming and how many pounds of trash I expect we'll pick up.

JADE
Did you guys see the *Teen People* story about Emma Gorgeese and Brad Hanssome?

JANA
Totally! She's not nearly cute enough for him. He's way hot!

JADE
My father works for, like, his recording studio, and my iTunes account automatically downloads anything by Brad.

LULU
You have your own iTunes?

JANA
Don't you?

Pop Girls giggle.

JADE
(way snobby voice)
Everyone downloads music. And tweets, Snapchats, Facebooks, IMs, Instagrams, and texts. It's called

communicating. It's for sure more interesting than photo science or whatever you were just talking about.

LULU
(confused)
I know I'm not the world's best technology user, but I'm not an alien. And I'm definitely learning about this stuff from you guys.

JADE
(robotic tone)
Now hear this: it's time for you to return to your weirdo planet.

Not thinking, Lulu licks the new cotton candy lip gloss she'd been wearing and then rubs it off with the back of her hand. She gobbles a few chips dunked in salsa from her lunch.

JANA
And, like, when you leave, take that food with you. It turns you into a salsa-breathing dragon.

LULU
(trying to recover from the unraveling of her new friendships)
Guys, I just thought we'd plan for the party this weekend.

JADE
There're lots of parties this weekend.

Cell phones go off. Jade and Jana reach into their purses, glance at their screens, then crack up. Jenna, who'd been sitting quietly, just sent them texts.

Lulu decides to get up before she drowns off the coast of Pop Girl Island.

SCENE 20: HOLLYWOODED

INT. MONOGRAMMIT—FRIDAY AFTER SCHOOL

Monogrammit is a tiny but stuffed store. They monogram anything, in any style. Colored spools of thread stand on white shelves lining a pink wall. Neatly stacked pajamas, slippers, cosmetic bags, pillows, scarves, and blankets wait, ready to be purchased and initialed.

Lulu scoops fun-size candy bars from a glass urn. She knows Sophia would love this place, especially hearing the sewing machines hum from the back of the store. Before she gets too s'bad, Lulu pushes this thought out of her head and pops a mini Mounds bar in her mouth.

Alexis, Elana, and the kind and creative storeowner, ELISA, examine the personalized waffle fabric slippers and plush robes Alexis ordered earlier that week.

ALEXIS
These are WAY adorable.

She holds up a pair of white slippers with "Jade" monogrammed in silver.

LULU

Can I see whose names we got?

ALEXIS

(ignoring Lulu and talking to Elisa)
These need to be wrapped in cellophane.

ELANA

We all help. Where's the ribbons?

Elisa ducks in back to find cellophane and raffia.

LULU

Lex, the Pop Girls were so mean to me today. They made
me feel like a freaky alien.

ALEXIS

Guess who's imagining things? YOU.

LULU

When girls crack mean jokes about you and play with
their cell phones, it's a message that you don't belong.

ALEXIS

No, the message is: get a cell phone!

LULU

Lex, those girls don't want to come to my party.

ALEXIS

They all RSVPed that they're coming.

Lulu, Elana, and Elisa get busy wrapping the slippers. Lulu tries to read each monogrammed name.

ALEXIS
(strolling around the store instead of wrapping)
And, Lu, you've gotta get over your babyish thing about having Linc and Fiona at your party.

LULU
(almost yelling)
That's the WHOLE reason why I agreed to this party in the first place!

Lulu stops wrapping and swallows hard to steady her voice.

LULU
(trying to sound calm)
You said Spa-tacular was the type of party Mom and Dad would come to! Geez peas! As if I even need a reason for my parents to come to my birthday party!
(pause)
Did you even ask them, Lex?

ELANA
(looking up from wrapping)
You both are in a *tienda*. Not your casa. Alexis, what's the story now? I know your parents are muy busy this weekend. They coming? Yes or no?

Jade and her mother, DANA DEVINE, enter the store before Alexis can answer.

LULU
(from behind the counter)

Oh, Jade, hi! I just saw your name on one of my party favors.

JADE
(quietly)

I don't think I'll be needing that.

Jade nervously glances toward her mother, who gives Jade a warning look. Lincoln Harrison might be winning an Academy Award in two days! She wants to tell people their daughters are "best friends."

Alexis observes Dana and figures out in a second: she's the type who's attracted to the rich and famous, like a moth to cashmere.

DANA
(to Lulu, who's tying raffia)

You look busy, sweetie.

JADE

You working here now? Trying to save this store or something?

LULU

No, just helping wrap party favors for, ya know, my birthday Spa-tacular.

DANA
(sugary sweet)

Oh, that reminds me. I came to get my tank tops

166

monogrammed for summer. But, darn, I forgot to
bring them.

Dana heads for the door.

> DANA
> Soooo super to see the Harrison girls. Fingers crossed
> for your dad! Tell him good luck!

Dana quickly walks out. Jade turns to follow.

Lulu comes out from behind the counter.

> LULU
> (calling after Jade)
> Your mom can tell him herself when she drops you off at
> my party on Sunday.

> JADE
> (spins around to face Lulu)
> You, Miss Brainy, can't seem to get the simplest clue. I'm
> not gonna be there! If only you read more *Teen People*
> and less science books, you'd know your dad's not gonna
> be there either. It's the ACADEMY AWARDS! Hellllo?!

Jade scurries out, clearly not wanting to confront Alexis, who'd
crept toward her like a cat stalking its prey.

> LULU
> So, Lex, NOW do you think I'm making myself feel like
> an alien?

ALEXIS

She's a tacky loser.

Instantly, Alexis's iPhone goes crazy. Texts, emails, and phone calls zing into her phone at the same time. Alexis glances at the screen and starts working her touchpad like a pro.

ALEXIS
(without looking up)
Elana, I need to get straight home, PLEASE!

LULU

What's happening? Who's calling? I wanna know what's going on!

ALEXIS
(distressed, continues typing)
Seems like Tara Falls, up-and-coming starlet of *Sweetest 16*, a new reality show that I know you've never watched, is throwing a pre-Academy Awards party. Same time and day as your Spa-tacular.

Elana grabs the box of personalized slippers then, on second thought, leaves the box on the counter. She thanks Elisa, telling her she'll be back on Saturday. Then, Elana, Lulu, and Alexis hustle to the car.

FADE OUT.

ACT III: L.A. FAMILY STYLE

SCENE 1: BIRTHDAY GONE BUST

EXT. HARRISON HOME—AN HOUR AFTER ARRIVING HOME FROM MONOGRAMMIT

Lulu sits on large stone steps just outside the front door of the neatly painted white brick house. Its dark green shutters look almost black in the last rays of afternoon sunlight. Lulu watches bees, birds, and butterflies flutter about enormous marble urns sprouting English lavender and Mexican sage.

Alexis exits the house and sits down next to Lulu. Neither sister talks. Lulu is lost in a trance, watching the natural world around her. Alexis is lost in a trance, sorting out the social world in her head.

After a while…

LULU

Watch those Monarch butterflies on the milkweed. I love hanging out with them 'cause they'd never be bothered by the drama going on in the house. I didn't want to be bothered, either.

ALEXIS

It was pretty noisy in there. Mega glad Linc and Fiona weren't home. An hour of everything ring-toning would have made them furious.

LULU

They'd be right.

ALEXIS

Plus, I would've been totally embarrassed. OMG, I would've died if they'd been home for this extremely nasty Hollywooding.

LULU
(turns to face Alexis)
What are you even talking about?

ALEXIS

Hollywooded. That's what you were. Big time!

LULU
(eyes wide with curiosity)
What?

ALEXIS

"Hollywooded" is when people cancel on you because a
better invitation comes along.

LULU

But I thought you got everything for Spa-tacular that Pop
Girls like? What invitation could be better?

ALEXIS

It's an invitation for a cooler party with better people.

LULU

It's the same people! All the girls canceled on me to go to
Tara Falls's party.

ALEXIS

Actually, someone named Jenna hasn't called yet.

LULU

Probably thinks I'm not even worth the effort to call.
All the Pop Girls and their followers climb into a boat
and row off to another location. Same people, just a
different place.

ALEXIS

(drawing a breath before delivering the final punch)
No, Lu. Tara Falls, the party hostess, is a reality TV
actress, and she's having stars come by.

CUT!! Don't you think this is *mucho* crazy nutty absurd? Really? If you were in my situation, would you laugh or cry? Back to: ACTION!!

LULU
(angry confusion in her voice)
Geez peas! I can't believe this! The Pop Girls wanna go to another party to see movie stars? The same day they could see my dad right here at my house? Right before he might win an Academy Award in front of millions of people worldwide?

Elana has been standing behind the girls throughout their conversation.

ELANA
Alexis, you tell your sister the whole story. *Todo!* In plain English so it's easy to understand. *Comprende?* I don't want nothing lost in the translation. You spill, *muchacha.*

ALEXIS
Linc and Fiona won't be at your party. Lulu, it's the ACADEMY AWARDS! And they're IN IT! Fiona's a presenter, and the movie she directed is up for Best Picture. Linc could win Best Actor. They've got hundreds of things to do to prepare: hair, makeup, fittings, photo shoots, and interviews.

LULU
(loud, angry voice)
You shoulda told me from the start. I would've ended this ridiculous party weeks ago.

(pause)

Is that why the Pop Girls aren't coming? Because they know Mom and Dad won't be here?

ALEXIS

Yep. You're finally applying your big brain. It seems Jana's father is an agent at Enduring, the same place as Steve, Dad's agent. Jana's dad told her that there's NO way Lincoln Harrison would be at your party because he'd be out all day getting ready for the Oscars.

LULU
(covering her ears)

I can't listen anymore.
(flooding anger)

Alexis, you're the worst party planner ever!

ALEXIS
(very quietly)

You're right.

LULU

You made my birthday into a soufflé that was guaranteed to flop 'cause it never went in the oven! You didn't even try to get Mom and Dad to come.

ALEXIS
(whispering)

You're right.

LULU
(yelling)
Now no one is coming! Pop Girls: zero! My best friend, Sophia: zero! Mom and Dad? Zero! It's because I'm a zero. How'd I let you talk me into this?
(pausing for breath)
I let this happen!

Lulu bends forward and grabs her knees trying to squeeze out the sloshing feeling in her tummy.

ALEXIS
No, Lu...

Alexis slides across the long step to be next to her sister.

ALEXIS
(sincerely)
I let this happen. I have no idea how to get Mom and Dad's attention on anything, either. I pretended that I could.

LULU
You pretended? But you made me think you'd get them to come. You were faking the whole time?

ALEXIS
Yup, I faked it.
(long pause)
OK, it's not what you think. At first, I imagined I could

plan something good enough that Mom and Dad would come. But as soon as I heard they were going to the Academy Awards, I knew they wouldn't come to your spa thing. That, actually, took pressure off me. I was, like, just planning a cool party. I don't know what came over me.
(takes a breath)
Lulu, I kinda forgot about you.

LULU

Kinda exactly like what Dad and Mom do.

ALEXIS
(rising anger)
Look, for your 411, they've never been to any of MY birthday parties either!

Lulu and Alexis turn and look at each other for the first time during this conversation. After a moment, both girls' eyes fill with tears. Lulu puts her head down in Alexis's lap. Alexis places her thin, manicured hand on Lulu's wild, uncombed hair.

ALEXIS
(sad voice)
OK, so that's it. Really, I'm awful, and I understand if you hate me forever. I get it if you release ladybugs in my room, or train the birds to peck me, or mix a chemical concoction that makes my hair fall out, or even teach Watson to poop in my Jimmy Choos...

ELANA
(putting an arm around both girls' shoulders)
Muy bien, Alexis. Good girl. See, Lulu, I tell you to trust your sister. She tell you the truth.

Lulu sits straight up, her green eyes wide with excitement.

LULU
Yeah, she's told me some very good ideas about how to get her back for this mess! I'm just not sure which I'm gonna do first.

All three giggle softly. Soon, they see Petal pull up the long driveway. She stops in front of them.

Revenge of the Lulu

SCENE 2: PARTY RESCUE

EXT. HOUSE FRONT STEPS / MOTOR COURT— CONTINUOUS

> PETAL

Peace, gals.

Petal pulls her shades down her nose and looks at Lulu and Alexis over the lenses.

> PETAL

Wow, long faces. Should be partying on. Academy Awards, and, Lady Lulu, it's almost your b-day!

> ALEXIS

That's exactly the problem. The Awards and Lulu's birthday are on the same day.

> PETAL

Hey, gals, joy up! At least you don't have to spend it driving around to zillions of parties, beauty appointments, publicity interviews, and airport pickups. Look at this schedule!

Petal flashes pages printed with times, locations, and contacts. The girls' eyes follow the flapping pages.

> LULU
> (suddenly excited)

Hey, Petal, you're mucho incredible, stupendous! Can I see that?

PETAL

Lulu, I know you're cool. You're not texting, tweeting, or
calling paparazzi. So you wanna see it? No problem, but
keep it away from that one.

Petal wiggles her forefinger at Alexis.

ALEXIS
(to Lulu)
Why do you want to see that?

PETAL
(winks at Lulu)
Lulu girl, you've always got a plan!

Cell phone rings inside the car. Petal answers. While listening,
she tosses the booklet of Linc and Fiona's weekend schedule into
the front seat. She soon disconnects.

PETAL

Seems that Stab and Slovinia's plane is landing early.
Gotta fly.

ALEXIS

Glamazon? She's here?

LULU

Who or what is Glamazon?

ALEXIS

She's only one of the world's top models. Slovinia is

called "the Glamazon" because she's a très-gorgeous, six-foot blond. It's rumored she's dating Stab.

> LULU
> (serious tone)
> Oh, well, if she's friends with Stab, I'll add her to my guest list.

Petal rises her darkened window as she glides the car down the driveway. Suddenly, her brake lights go on. Petal backs up, rolls down her window, and hands Lulu an oversized, overstuffed envelope.

SCENE 3: PLAN OF ACTION

INT. ALEXIS'S BEDROOM—CONTINUOUS

Minutes after Petal's departure, Lulu grabs Alexis and yanks her upstairs. Alexis doesn't invite Lulu into her room, but given the mess she'd created, she doesn't complain now when Lulu barges in.

Alexis loved having Fiona's fancy decorator "do" her room. Slate blue walls match the rest of the house. Nothing is personalized, except her clothes and shoes strewn about the antique silk carpet. Crisp, monogrammed sheets cover her queen-sized bed. Cream-and-blue-striped drapes hang around the bed, sham-covered pillows are placed across the headboard. A flatscreen TV is framed onto a wall. Silver-framed black and white publicity photographs of her parents surround the room.

LULU

Have I ever told you, Lex, that you're a talented actress?

ALEXIS

Excuse me?

LULU

You've got all of Mom's mucho glam style, but, no offense
to your party planning skills, you're a better actress
than director.

ALEXIS

What's your point? We're facing mega social suicide
here. NOT a good time for compliments.

LULU

From now on, I'm the writer and director, and I'm
giving you a script. Here's the project: Hosting the most
amazing Spa-tacular party!

ALEXIS

Stop joking. I've got "humiliation" with a giant H on
my forehead.

Focused on her own thoughts, Lulu ignores Alexis.

LULU

All my friends and family will be there. I'll handle all
the guests, except two: Mom and Dad. That's where you
come in.

ALEXIS

Really, I think we should just get Elana to drive us to Santa Barbara for the weekend. We can hide out there.

LULU

What are you talking about? You're gonna be Mom and Dad's new assistant this weekend.

Alexis tugs nervously on the ends of her silky, perfect hair.

LULU

No one else could play this part! You've got the style and smarts to be the confident, invaluable assistant to Hollywood's Power Couple.

ALEXIS
(interested, but confused)
But they have assistants, remember? Lilac and Leif! Helllllllo?!

LULU

Right! Here's the plan. One: Linc's and Fiona's assistants are going to be busy with Stab and the Glamazon. That's a trick up my sleeve. Two: for an hour tomorrow afternoon, you're THE I'm-so-important-because-I-do-errands-for-a-celebrity assistant.

ALEXIS

What am I even supposed to do?

> LULU

Here's your script!

With a flourish, Lulu tosses a booklet to Alexis. It's a copy of her parents' weekend schedule with a big red "CONFIDENTIAL" scribbled across the top. Little red writing scrawled at the bottom says, "Happy B-day, xoxo Petal."

Alexis flips through the twenty-five pages. She can't believe what she's looking at.

> ALEXIS
> (stunned)

This is Linc and Fiona's 411! It's every place they're going and for how long...addresses, contacts, EVERYTHING. You can't have this!

> LULU

Chill, it's OK, I'm sure Petal has another copy.

> ALEXIS

But it's their private, personal schedule!

> LULU

When did YOU become a Girl Scout? I know you once told your friend, Sharon Lime, when Dad was taking a tennis lesson, and she snuck a picture of him and sold it to *Starz* magazine.

Alexis is struck silent. She's been whacked into total embarrassment by her little, messy, salsa-stinking sister.

182

LULU

OK, here's the deal. You're gonna cancel ALL of Mom and Dad's Sunday appointments—hair, nails, gown and tuxedo fitting, interviews, the works! Everything goes, EXCEPT, of course, the Academy Awards.

ALEXIS
(stunned)

What?! You're living up to your name and going totally lulu!

LULU
(ignoring the remark)

Anything they need to do to get ready, we'll have covered here...
(waves her hand around)
...at the Spa-tacular.

ALEXIS

How do I tell Linc and Fiona that their appointments are canceled?

LULU

Your script doesn't call for telling them anything. Your role is the snobby, high and mighty assistant. If you happen to run into Mom and Dad, you say nada! To them, you play the boyfriend-and-shopping-crazed teen daughter. That should be easy for you.

ALEXIS

Shouldn't I remind them about your birthday?

> LULU

Don't be a goof. Think in character, Lex! Would a way-cool, busy teenage sister bother about her little sister's birthday?

> ALEXIS

Good point.

> LULU

Thanks. I know.

Alexis examines the many-page schedule.

> LULU

Oh, and I'll make sure you get co-producing credit, OK?

Alexis tosses the schedule booklet back to Lulu. It makes her uneasy just to hold it.

> ALEXIS

Look, Lu, I'm more than a little worried about what you're asking.

> LULU

It's a great part! You're lucky to have landed it. Right now, concentrate on your acting.
>
> (pause)
>
> All good roles are challenging, Lex. Now I've gotta go.
>
> (heads toward door)
>
> Geez peas! No wonder Mom's always busy. Directing

means putting tons of little puzzle pieces together to make one great picture.

Almost at the door, Lulu turns back to Alexis.

LULU

Just so you stop worrying...I'm gonna reach Stab and ask him to call Linc's and Fiona's real assistants, Lilac and Leif. He'll tell them to get to Chateau Marmont ASAP to keep snooping reporters away from him and Glamazon. Oh, and he'll warn them not to bring their cell phones so they can't be tracked by the paparazzi.

ALEXIS

That's supposed to make me STOP worrying?!!

LULU

That time I met Stab, he said I could call him.

ALEXIS

Lu, how do YOU even know Hollywood stuff, like producing, directing, scripts, credits, paparazzi?

LULU

You think I'm a geeky nerd, but that doesn't make me completely spacey about the family business...because, well, I've been part of this family my whole life.

Lulu pushes unbrushed hair from her face then exits.

SCENE 4: GET IN TOUCH WITH MY PEOPLE

INT. HARRISONS' POOL CABANA—SATURDAY MORNING, 8:00 A.M.

Lulu zooms into the pool house where she's arranged a secret meeting with Elana, Johnny Walker, Hernandez, and Chip.

> LULU
> (cheery)
>
> Hey, guys! Good morning!

> ELANA
>
> Niña, is this gonna take long? I can make coffee.

> LULU
> (clearing throat)
>
> No, not long. Ahhummm... Sorry to beg you all to come here so early, but I wanted to let you know I've taken over my birthday!

Lulu stops to watch her pals glance at one another.

> LULU
>
> You see, Alexis and I are now co-producers of my party. And, now that I'm involved, there'll be some changes. I want to have my OWN people. It's key to the success of the entire project.

JOHNNY
Hey, this is really cool. Lulu is channeling Fiona.

Muffled chuckles ripple through room.

LULU
Actually, I'm just tapping into another part of the real Lulu.

Walking up to each person, Lulu hands out cards with dried flowers pasted on the front.

LULU
I was up very late hand-making these...

All are quiet while they study their handmade invitations.

HERNANDEZ
This is muy *bonita*. And *mi familia*? I can bring my girls?

LULU
Of course, Hernandez. I personally invite you all to my birthday party tomorrow at eleven a.m.
(pauses)
Lately, I'd lost sight of who my friends are. I forgot who teaches and helps me. I forgot who makes me laugh and makes me safe. You're all the greatest friends an almost-eleven-year-old could have. So, please, and por favor, come tomorrow as my honored VIP, five-star, numero uno guests!

JOHNNY
(stands up)
I shall be there, Miss Lulu, with bells on.

Johnny makes a long, sweeping bow.

LULU
Johnny, awesome, but ummmm, please don't wear anything with bells.

JOHNNY
(winking at Lulu)
Ooooh, you got me!

All chuckle.

JOHNNY
I'm going to bathe Watson and find him something snazzy to wear. We'll arrive looking like a million bucks!

LULU
Well, that reminds me. It's a spa party. I don't really know what that means, but prepare to be pampered.

CHIP
You mean diapered, like Watson?

More giggles from the gang.

LULU
Ya know, spa stuff. Like oiled, scrubbed, and polished. So just wear comfy clothes.

CHIP
I surf Sunday mornings. OK if I come sorta sandy?

LULU
The sandier the better!

HERNANDEZ
(gets up)
OK. I gotta go because I want to make the grounds look perfecto!

LULU
Everything already looks perfecto, Hernandez. Please don't worry about it. And, Chip, that goes for you too.

Watson trudges in looking disheveled and smelling stinky as usual.

LULU
Actually, Johnny, the pooping pug needs some work.

Everyone reacts to the odor then gets up to leave.

LULU
Does anyone have time to get to Mr. Garza's truck today? I have an invitation for him and Miguel.

Chip, Johnny, and Hernandez all offer to deliver the invitation. They plan to meet at the truck for a delicious midday lunch. Lulu hands the invitation to Chip.

LULU
(to Chip)
Please tell them not to bring anything. Just come to celebrate.

Chip gives a little salute then, quietly, into her ear…

CHIP
You make a really cool mini director. You can cast me in your projects any time!
(pauses)
Hey, I have a script I might want you to read for me.

Lulu gives Chip an overly dramatic wink. They both crack up.

ELANA
(to Lulu)
I love my invitation. The painted sky and the pressed-down flora. I put this in a frame.

LULU
Gracias, Momny. See, they were all different.

Lulu holds out other invitations painted with different backgrounds. One is pressed petals in the shape of a peace sign, the other a bluebell.

ELANA

Who are those for?

LULU

Oh, well, ummmm, they're harder to deliver. One's for
Petal, but she's so busy.

ELANA

Give me that one. I do it for you. She's driving back and
forth to the casa all day for your parents.

LULU

Well, that's just it. I don't want my parents to know
anything about this.

ELANA

No problemo. I take care of it. Who the other
invitation for?

LULU

Sophia.

ELANA
(serious look)
Ahh, that one, niña, you gotta do by yourself.

SCENE 5: BUGGING SOPHIA

**EXT. HARRISON PROPERTY, OUTSIDE THE ENTRANCE
GATE—SATURDAY**

Lulu has set up a bug stand right on Stone Canyon Road. A white tablecloth covers a small table. On top of the table are various-sized jars, each containing bugs. A large hand-drawn sign in front advertises the sale of caterpillars and ladybugs. Lulu sits behind the table reading a book but looks up each time a car zooms by, which isn't too often in her exclusive neighborhood. Drivers don't even touch their brakes when passing her bug stand.

Finally, a car cruises over and stops. It's Officer Gale from Bel-Air Patrol. He gets out and approaches Lulu.

> OFFICER GALE
> Good afternoon, Lulu!

> LULU
> Hi, Officer Gale. I'm safe. I'm not sticking too far into the street. Did someone complain about me?

> OFFICER GALE
> (radio crackles inside patrol car)
> Elana.

> LULU
> She knows where I am. I promised not to get out of camera range.

Lulu points up at the security cameras perched on tall gateposts in front of the Harrison driveway.

OFFICER GALE

Sure, she was watching you from the house. But she can't sit and monitor you all day.

Officer Gale walks over to her bug table. He picks up a jar.

OFFICER GALE

So, how's the bug business?

LULU

Let's just say the bugs aren't flying off the table.

OFFICER GALE

Hey, Hernandez called me to say he was bringing you a hive of honeybees. Asked if there's a rule against beekeeping in Bel-Air.

LULU
(excited to talk about bugs)
Bees are the best! They pollinate everything we grow and eat. My best friend, Sophia, and I are gonna get their honey next spring.

OFFICER GALE

Well, I'll be ready for the 911 call when you guys go for the honey. Bees aren't good at sharing.

LULU
(giggling)
We'll be fine. We have some great bug books.

Lulu holds up a copy of *Bug Me* that she's been reading.

OFFICER GALE
(returning a jar of ladybugs to the table)
So why are you de-bugging now?

LULU
Well, ummm. I'm trying to get Sophia to stop here. She doesn't want to be my friend anymore because I didn't invite her to my birthday party.

OFFICER GALE
Didn't invite your best friend to your birthday party? I don't copy that.

LULU
I acted like a jerk and a chicken and never told her to come.

OFFICER GALE
Got it.
(pauses)
Well, happy birthday, Lulu. I hope you two work it out.

LULU
Thank you, Officer Gale. Would you like to come tomorrow? It's at eleven a.m.

OFFICER GALE
I'd love to, but I gotta check with Mrs. Gale.

                    LULU
She should come too!

                 OFFICER GALE
Roger that. We'll both be there.
                    (thinks a moment)
See how easy it is?

                    LULU
What's easy?

                 OFFICER GALE
Just saying what you mean. To the point. From the heart.

A car slows down.

                 OFFICER GALE
Looks like you finally got a customer.

                    LULU
That's Sophia and her mom!

                 OFFICER GALE
Well, don't sit there looking like you swallowed a fly.

Eve's yellow Mini Cooper pulls up to the Harrisons' gates. The
driver's window comes down. Eve pushes the buzzer to get in.
While the gate slowly swings open, Eve waves.

EVE

Hi, Lulu! I'm here to work on your mom. I'm sensing she has very tense shoulders today.

Lulu bites her bottom lip then glances at Officer Gale, who casually leans against his patrol car.

OFFICER GALE

Just the facts, Lulu.

LULU
(turning to the yellow car)
Is Sophia with you?

Eve looks behind her.

LULU

I'd mucho like to talk to her! You see, I was out here selling bugs, but what I was really doing was waiting for you to come over 'cause I was hoping she'd come with you.

Sophia wiggles herself from the car's tiny back seat and steps out.

SOPHIA

Hi, Lulu. Are you selling the ladybugs we just released?

LULU

Ummmm, yes. Well, it's too soon to be their larvae already.

The patrol radio zzzuzzes and crackles. Officer Gale twists buttons on his radio to get Lulu's attention. She looks over and sees him tap the badge pinned over his heart.

> LULU
> (directed at Officer Gale)
> Right. Got it.
> (back to Sophia)
> To be honest, I'm out here to tell you that...

Lulu takes a rare breath between words.

> LULU
> I'm sorry I was a weakling and a jerk and I let myself be bossed around by Queen Bee and, well, more than anything in the world, I want you to come to my birthday party tomorrow.

Sophia doesn't respond or move an inch.

> LULU
> It's not exactly the party you and I planned, but it'll be fun. And, well, if you're not there, my eleven will just be "one" without the other "one."

Sophia is still frozen.

> LULU
> OK, Sophia, just say yes or I'm gonna keep bugging you!

Sophia smiles.

> **SOPHIA**
>
> You're pretending to sell garden insects on the streets of Bel-Air just to get me to know you're still my best friend? How could I resist that?

Lulu races over to hug her friend and hand her the homemade invitation tucked between the pages of *Bug Me*.

> **SOPHIA**
>
> C'mon. Let's go release these guys. The ladybugs and caterpillars are probably starving.

> **LULU**
>
> I am too!

Lulu pops Officer Gale a thumbs-up.

SCENE 6: OPERATION CANCELLATION

INT. ALEXIS'S BEDROOM—4:00 P.M. SATURDAY AFTERNOON

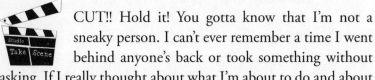 CUT!! Hold it! You gotta know that I'm not a sneaky person. I can't ever remember a time I went behind anyone's back or took something without asking. If I really thought about what I'm about to do and about what I'm making Alexis do, I might not do it. Sometimes, though, every so often, probably around the time you're about to be eleven, you gotta let your heart take over from your head.

My desire to have my family together for my birthday over-powers my thoughts of *I could be killed for what I'm about to do.*

I'm like those people who climb into giant trees to prevent loggers with chainsaws from cutting them down. It's not exactly right for them to be in the trees because the trees don't belong to them. But their feelings take over, and they do something really important, like save a tree that has strong, deep roots and has been part of the earth for longer than anyone has been alive. So, now's my turn to save my family tree. Back to: ACTION!!

Lulu turns Alexis's room into Operation Cancellation Headquarters.

LULU

(sounding very in charge)

OK. We've got about one hour. According to their schedule, Mom and Dad nap till five o'clock.

ALEXIS

I think I'm dreaming.

LULU

(charging ahead)

We just need a couple of importante props.

ALEXIS

The stress has given me a headache. The prop I need right now is aspirin.

199

Lulu paces around the room.

> LULU
>
> The key to being convincing is to call everyone from Dad and Mom's personal cell phones.

> ALEXIS
>
> You're joking, right? You've eaten a rotten chip or some spoiled salsa.

> LULU
>
> This is the perfect time to nab their phones.

> ALEXIS
>
> We can't swipe their stuff!

> LULU
>
> Oh! And, geez peas! Forgot to tell ya. Jenna should be here any second to help. In case we can't find any phone numbers, Jenna said she has direct numbers for lots of exclusive places.

> ALEXIS
>
> It's like I can't process the words you're saying!

> LULU
>
> Well, since Jenna never called me, I called her. Turns out, she's still coming. And is super nice. She's a real amiga. She asked what she could do.

ALEXIS

I'm talking about your whole insane plan. We do this and Linc and Fiona will be: send-these-girls-to-boarding-school-in-Switzerland-without-a-sweater FURIOUS!

Lulu quits pacing stares at Alexis.

LULU
(in a serious, firm voice)
First, your name is all over my Spa-tacular party. If it's a big zonker, it'll be all over twitters, Facebooks, or whatever. You'll go down with the ship. Second, you owe me big time. You made a mess of things.
(softening)
Last, Lex, I can't do this without you, but we can do this together. Really!

ALEXIS
(mostly talking to herself)
It's coming into focus. If Linc and Fiona DO show up—

Alexis nervously picks nail polish off her thumb.

LULU
Not to mention Stab and Glamazon. They'll be at my party too!

ALEXIS
(looking right at Lulu)
OK. But let me just say it better work!

(to herself)
I can't believe I'm gonna do this insane plan!

INT. LINC AND FIONA'S BEDROOM—CONTINUOUS

The girls sneak into their parents' bedroom. They hear Linc's loud, powerful snoring and can't help cracking up. They cover their mouths to muffle giggles.

The bedroom's electric shades are down. It's as pitch black as a big cave. Their parents wear those weird satin eye masks, like they need that too!

Alexis and Lulu shuffle in the direction of their parents' closets. They reach Fiona's first.

ALEXIS
(whispering)
Every time I come in here, I can't believe how gigantic this closet is. It's like an apartment!

Lulu flicks on the petite crystal chandelier and shuts the door.

ALEXIS
Oh, look over there, the purse Fiona carried today.
(picking up purse)
It's full!

Alexis rummages through her mother's purse.

ALEXIS
(still whispering)
Jackpot!

Alexis holds up Fiona's iPhone then quickly slides it into her pocket.

Lulu shuts off her mom's closet light, wedges open the door, and soundlessly tiptoes into her dad's closet. Alexis follows.

LULU
I'll check Dad's jeans and jacket from today.

The phone isn't there. The girls scramble, frantically bumping into each other and dropping clothes on the floor.

ALEXIS
Oh, Lu, we're running out of time. If we don't find his phone ASAP, there won't be enough time to cancel anything!

Panic creeps into Alexis's voice. She's feeling defeated after looking through what seems like eight hundred of Linc's pockets.

LULU
Geez peas! I have a great idea! Let's call Dad's cell phone. We'll hear the ring and know where it is.

Alexis pulls her mom's phone from her pocket and dials. They hear the national anthem (Linc's ring tone), but it's coming from the bedroom! They race out of the closet and see Linc's cell phone flashing on his bedside table.

Lulu and Alexis freeze and hold their breath. Linc turns over, ignoring the music. It stops. Lulu dives for the iPhone, grabs it, and tosses it to Alexis.

The sisters crawl out of their parents' room. Giddy with excitement, they high-five each other then head down the long hall, prized cell phones wedged into Alexis's pants pockets.

Steps from their parent's bedroom, they hear *CLONK* and then *CLATTER*! Fiona's cell phone skids across the polished wood floor like a puck on ice.

ALEXIS
(panicked whisper)

It popped out!

LULU
(gasping)

UHHHHHH! It's about to hit...

Watson lies down in the phone's path. Instead of plowing into their parent's bedroom door, the iPhone thuds into Watson's chubby, furry side, barely making a sound.

LULU
(trying not to giggle)

Come, Watson.

Watson claps his mouth around the iPhone and waddles behind Lulu and Alexis.

INT. BACK INSIDE ALEXIS' ROOM—CONTINUOUS

> LULU

Ready, Lex?

There's a soft knock on the door. Jenna shyly walks in. Lulu bounces over, hugs her, then hands her a list.

> LULU
> (to Jenna)

Know any of these places?

> JENNA
> (quickly scanning the list)

Sure. I've been to them all. Everyone gets their eyebrows waxed at Anastasia and—

> LULU

MUCHO deluxe! Just write down the phone numbers next to each place, and then Alexis will call it!

Jenna yanks out her phone and gets going. She's scrolling and scribbling in, like, twenty seconds.

> LULU

Ready, Lex? You gotta make the calls in your best grownup voice.

Alexis draws a deep breath while Lulu dials the first number. When it starts to ring, Lulu hands Alexis the phone.

ALEXIS
(snotty British accent)
Calling for Fiona Harrison! Is this Fredric speaking?
Fiona will not be seeing you tomorrow at eleven a.m. She's
moved on at this point. Thank you.

Alexis pauses a moment to listen to the angry response. Fredric
cannot believe that his mega client, Hollywood's hottest female
director, just canceled on him.

ALEXIS
(still in accent)
I'm sure you don't want me to repeat what you just
said, sir. So I will simply tell Mrs. Harrison that you
wish her good luck on winning Best Picture tomorrow.
Good afternoon!

Alexis clicks off the call. Girls erupt in laughter.

LULU
What'd he say?

ALEXIS
It wasn't pretty.

LULU
OK, we got seven more to do just for Mom.

Lulu dials another number. She's Alexis's director—coaching, advis-
ing, and encouraging her sister the whole way through. Jenna keeps
the phone numbers coming. The girls are having the best time of

their lives. Alexis's British accent becomes more convincing with each call. Together, the girls undo the most difficult-to-get hair, makeup, and nail appointments, especially impossible to get on Oscar Day!

They also cancel interviews and photo sessions with reporters from all over the world. Through organization and perfect cooperation, the girls finish in forty-seven minutes flat.

Now, the hard part: sneaking the phones back into their parents' bedroom by 5:00 p.m. Oh, and getting themselves back out!

JENNA
(flashing a perfect, white, toothy smile)
Hate to dial and dash but, I told you Lu, I'm going to the Tyler Sure concert tonight. And with my mom! Geeky, right?

LULU
NO that's awesome! Mega gracias for helping.

JENNA
(giving Lulu a one-armed hug)
You guys are gonna rock this thing.

INT. HALLWAY OUTSIDE LINC AND FIONA'S BEDROOM—CONTINUOUS

LULU
There are only a few minutes before Mom and Dad are conscious.

Lulu holds the cell phones tightly in her hands, as if squeezing hard enough might make them disappear.

> LULU
>
> Here's the plan. You race into Mom's closet, toss her iPhone into her purse, and fly back out. I'll take care of Dad's phone.

Lulu cracks open the bedroom door and shoves willowy Alexis through the opening.

> LULU
> (panicked whisper)
>
> Wait!

Lulu pulls Alexis back by her belt loop.

> LULU
>
> Take off your shoes! They make too much cloppity-clop noise.

Alexis kicks off her bright green Jenni Kayne mules. Lulu sends her back through the bedroom door. Like a gazelle, Alexis leaps across the huge bedroom and disappears into Fiona's dressing area. She plunks the phone back into the purple Hermès bag then begins her retreat.

Seeing Alexis sprint out, Lulu creeps in the room.

Close up on Lulu as she steadies her aim, concentrates on her target, then releases. Her dad's iPhone skitters across the bedroom floor and slows to a stop right next to his bedside table. Alexis freezes, watching Lulu's perfect shot.

LULU
(loud whisper)
C'mon! Get out of therrrr...

An alarm peals *PLING, PLING, TING, TING*! It's from Fiona's small oval Cartier clock perched on her nightstand. Its alarm sounds like someone whacking the Eiffel Tower with a metal rod.

Alexis slides out the bedroom door. Lulu clicks it shut just as the alarm ceases. The girls grab each other and burst into laughter.

 CUT!! Again, sorry, I know you want to see what happens next, but this is important. Pulling this party from the scrap heap has been a growing experience. And it doesn't even hurt, like when you get an achy leg and some adult tells you it's just growing pains.

And WOW! Note to self: consider trying out for the U.S. Olympic curling team. Wouldn't that show all those Crosswinds kids who think I'm the ultimate worst klutz ever?! Back to: ACTION!!

SCENE 7: GOING, GOING FINALLY GONE

EXT. HARRISON'S FRONT ENTRANCE AND MOTOR COURT—EARLY SUNDAY MORNING

Tired and bedraggled from the hoopla festivities of the night before, Fiona and Linc stand nervously, waiting for Petal to pick them up and take them to Oscar-day appointments.

Alexis and Lulu spy on their parents from the window of Alexis's ginormous bathroom, which is strewn with hair products, nail polish, makeup, body lotions, and perfume bottles—all waiting for pre-party use.

> LULU
> (loud whisper)
> Petal should be here by now. She's probably stuck in line at Caffe Luxxe.

> ALEXIS
> (worried)
> Linc and Fiona better get out of here. The tent, flowers, food—everything's about to pull up right in front of them.

> LULU
> We better distract them! They gotta stay totally spaced out that it's my Spa-tacular. I don't want them to suspect anything when their morning starts to go, well, mucho wrong!

Lulu and Alexis race downstairs. Lulu reaches the bottom of the stairs first. Hair flying, face red, and panting, Lulu bursts through the front door.

> LULU
> Bye, Mom and Dad. Have a great day. See ya...soon.

Lulu smiles her sweetest smile because she knows they'll be back before they know it.

ALEXIS
(now also outside)
Yipes! You guys look wiped. You better get transformed on the double!

Hidden behind very oversized sunglasses, Linc and Fiona manage weak, tired smiles in response. At that moment, Petal pulls up and the couple drops into the back seat. Petal hands each of them a soy vanilla latte.

LULU
(to Alexis)
I can't take this anymore. They've gotta go!

Petal hits the gas as soon as Lulu's "go" is spoken. The girls watch their parents zoom down the driveway.

ALEXIS
That was WAY stressful. I'm gonna faint.

LULU
Well, there's no time. Look!

A truck chugs up the long driveway. Alexis dashes off to direct it.

ALEXIS
(arms waving)
Hey, park over here! Don't run over any fancy English roses.

> LULU

Hey, don't forget the bugs! If he squashes those rose bushes, he'll kill a world of ladybugs living under the leaves!

The truck comes to a safe stop around the side of the house. Petals and pests are spared.

> LULU
> (bursting with excitement)
> Geez peas! It's my *compleaños*. I wanna start celebrating!

> ALEXIS

Well, you may want to chill on that for a moment.
> (pauses and points at Lulu)

You're still wearing your pajamas!

Lulu lets out a loud "AHHHHH" and scampers into the house.

SCENE 8: LET'S GET THIS PARTY STARTED

EXT. HARRISON DRIVEWAY and GRASSY LAWN—10:00 A.M.

Now wearing their party outfits, Lulu and Alexis return to the action. Alexis looks runway-ready in a mega-short, form-fitting, hot pink scalloped strapless Herve Leger dress and towering, suede, beaded Prada platform sandals complete with hand-sewn crystals. She's fully accessorized with gold and silver bangles.

The Harrison grounds are a hive of activity—food, flowers, tables, and chairs, moving in all directions. Alexis plays her role as party planner *extraordinaire*. She's Queen Bee at her finest, telling people where to go and what to do. Lulu bops around handing out frosted lemon bars and chatting with every person.

Soon, Lulu watches a great white party tent rise. She dashes over to Alexis.

> **LULU**
> Lex, seeing that tent come to life reminds me of those bouncy houses I used to have at my birthday parties. Remember? They'd be limp on the ground and within minutes...poof! They'd blow up huge!

> **ALEXIS**
> Hmmmmm, I confess...
> (looking right at Lulu)
> I don't remember actually going to any of your birthday parties before.

> **LULU**
> No prob. Eleven's a perfecto time for you to start coming.

Lulu grabs Alexis's wrist and pulls her inside the tent.

> **LULU**
> C'mon. Let's see inside!

INT. PARTY TENT—CONTINUOUS

The top of the tent is clear, letting in the natural sunlight. White orchids and tulle cover tables. Ivy is wrapped around the sides of the tent. There are five hundred balloons tied to silky white ribbons. The whole tent is scented with lavender tea candles.

In the corner, musicians warm up on guitar, bongos, and bamboo flute. Seeing Lulu, they break into a snappy version of "Happy Birthday."

> LULU
> (twirling around)
> It's like a fairyland! I wanna go and grab silk wings from my playroom attic.

Lulu flaps her arms.

> ALEXIS
> Stop! You look très chic in what you're wearing. And, before you go flying off, check out the surprise color.

Lulu's green eyes instantly dart from one table to another. Bright orange California poppies gracefully stand in small glass vases.

> LULU
> You used my favorite native wildflower in my FAVORITE color!

> ALEXIS
> Jennifer, from Floral Art, thought of it...after I finally decided to break the serene white theme with a touch of pure Lulu.

INT. SPA TENT—5 MINUTES LATER

Josette, Director of the Bel-Air Hotel Spa, arrives with her team of employees, who wear white lab coats and have bright, glowing skin. They frantically set up spa stations: massage tables, facial steamers, and small tables covered with every potion and lotion known to man or woman.

Lulu uncaps and smells all the creams. She quizzes the spa staff about the ingredients.

The very elegant, French Josette, with her hair in a French twist, swoops over to Lulu so her employees can work.

JOSETTE

Ma cherie Lulu. Excited about this celebration?

Josette does that kissy on each cheek thing to Lulu.

JOSETTE

Alexis tell me that you and nature—amour, amour! All our fantastique products you and your friends will be sampling are made from environmentally happy, organic, biodynamic ingredients.

LULU

Really? Alexis told you that? Well, like my fave tote bag says, "Save Earth. It's the only planet with chocolate."

Lulu hears her name. She looks up and sees Sophia walking toward her. Lulu, despite her fancy outfit and neatly combed hair, runs at

215

full speed. Sophia thrusts a lumpy package into Lulu's arms. With her own arms now free, she gives Lulu a tight hug.

SOPHIA
Happy birthday, Lu.
(Sophia looks around the tent)
Look at the flowers and candles. Everything's so beautiful.

LULU
(halting, unsure of Sophia's words)
Really, you like it? You don't think it's, ya know, too glitzy-glammy?

SOPHIA
It's really magical!
(in a serious, quiet voice)
Lulu, this is the fanciest party I've ever been to, and it's perfect that it's for my best friend's birthday.

Lulu hands Sophia back the lumpy gift and gives her friend a hug.

Sophia is dressed hippie chic in leggings (which look great on her because she's a beanpole) and a billowy floral print dress. And her major dress-up item: plastic ballet flats instead of her Converse sneakers. She looks perfect.

SOPHIA
Oh, I know this isn't the kind of party where a homemade gift is what you're supposed to bring, but, well, I did anyway.

Lulu nabs the gift back. She rips off the orange tissue paper.

When the paper falls away, Lulu holds up a small, pretty, patch-work blanket.

SOPHIA

It's scraps of our old clothes. It's a friendship blanket. I meant for it to be bigger but stopped working on it when...ya know, that week we didn't really talk. So it just came out this size.

LULU
(roaring with joy)

This is the most perfecto gift ever! It'll be our picnic blanket! We'll really use this, Soph! And it's SO like you, not another in the universe!

ELANA
(seeing the blanket)

Muy bonita! I remember all those clothes you have patches from!

Jenna walks up behind Lulu and Sophia and puts her arms around their shoulders.

JENNA
(playfully)

Boo!

LULU

Hey. You came!

JENNA
Promise is a promise. And besides, I know the food here is gonna be fantabulous!

Jenna looks hyper cool girl in layered tank tops over a zebra-striped miniskirt. She angles the arm draped around Lulu's shoulder to crook pinkies and cement the pinkie promise. Sophia looks confused, maybe even a bit hurt.

Chip comes up to the girls. He's sandy and damp from the ocean.

CHIP
Great! A towel! Just what I need!

Chip reaches for Sophia's gift. Lulu yanks it away.

LULU
(laughs)
It's not a towel! Sophia made it for my birthday.

JENNA
(looking at Sophia)
That rocks. You made it?

CHIP
(still mock grabbing)
Not a towel for me? Kidding. Happy birthday, gnarly Lulu! Hey, check out who was also out surfing this morning. Hope it's cool that he's in for the bash.

Robbie shuffles up to Lulu and musses her hair.

> ROBBIE
> (joking to Chip)
> Dude, this Lulu had her sister so busy yesterday that
> she canceled our date.

> LULU
> Ooops.

> CHIP
> Hey, man, can't stay sore at a girl named Lulu.

Everyone laughs. Chip and Robbie give Lulu birthday fist bumps.

Hernandez and his family arrive, as does Johnny Walker with Watson in tow. They swallow Lulu up in hugs, presents, and ooohs and aaahs about how the party tent looks.

Everyone pulls back to notice the snazzily dressed Watson. Despite his very English name, the pug sports a very French outfit—orange and fuchsia striped cashmere sweater and an orange beret. Not to be out-dressed by a dog, Johnny Walker wears an orange velvet jacket and a fuchsia beret. He's got a vintage The Who T-shirt underneath his jacket.

Officer and Mrs. Gale's arrival is announced by the patrol car's siren. Officer Gale snaps it on and off as he drives up to the party tent entrance.

EXT. HARRISON GROUNDS—CONTINUOUS

The unmistakable smell of frying tortilla chips wafts through the tent. The musical *toot* from the Garzas' taco truck follows just moments behind the scent.

Lulu can't believe her eyes! She dashes across the long lawn and bounces alongside the Garzas' shiny silver truck chugging up the Harrison driveway. She's waving her arms as if trying to stop a runaway horse.

The Taco Truck rolls to a stop.

Mr. Garza and Miguel jump out. Within minutes, they've opened the truck and set out bags of hot, fresh, homemade chips and mega-sized bowls of salsa.

MR. GARZA
(bellows)
Feliz compleaños, Señorita Lulu!

MIGUEL
Happy b-day!

Mr. Garza smothers Lulu in a bear hug then hands her a flower-shaped *piñata*. Miguel gives Lulu a brand-new football.

SOPHIA
(teasing)
Miguel! You gave Lulu a football? Ya know she's never caught one of those in her life!

MIGUEL

Hey, it's like, the only thing I could think of that she didn't have in this house!

LULU

I love it, Miguel!

MR. GARZA
(climbing back into truck)
Niña, Lulu! Now I gotta fry up more chips for your fiesta!

LULU
(follows him into the truck)
Oh, Señor Garza, are you using up food you should be selling? Miguel says maybe you can't keep the truck.

SENOR GARZA

Today is mi amiga Lulu's birthday. Making food for her is exactly what this truck is for.

Lulu bends down to get bowls and baskets for Mr. Garza as a way to hide her tiny tears about to leak out.

Alexis dashes over.

ALEXIS
(freaking out)
Lu, everyone is arriving sooooo early. The food buffet isn't done! Should guests start their spa treatments? Josette!

(yelling in half panic/half nerves)
Josette! Is everything ready?

Lulu jumps out of Mr. Garza's truck.

LULU

Lex, seems like everything's under control. Chillax. Hey,
let's just be guests instead of party planners, OK? At least
till Mom and Dad arrive. Then I don't know what we'll be—

ALEXIS

In megaton trouble! That's what we'll be.

Chip and Elana walk by, chatting and chuckling. They're wearing
soft robes with a ladybug patch on the left side.

Chip gives Lulu "OK" signs with his hands.

LULU

(to Alexis)
Hey, what's that they've got on?

ALEXIS

Oh, another surprise! I asked Elisa at Monogrammit to
sew ladybugs on all the robes and butterflies over the
formerly monogrammed slippers.

LULU

She did all THAT?!

ALEXIS

Sure. Elana made a secret run for everything last night.

LULU

Geez peas! This party must've made people, well, lulu!
(watching someone wander up the driveway)
I can't believe it! I think that's Mr. Ling!

ALEXIS

The Crosswinds science teacher?

Sophia approaches Lulu, spots Mr. Ling, and waves him over.

SOPHIA
(to Lulu)

Oh, I invited him.
(giggling)
I know Mr. Ling's been your favorite teacher since third
grade.

Lulu leaps toward Mr. Ling then introduces him to her friends.
Jenna tries to talk him into a facial. Just then, Miguel joins the group.

MIGUEL
(challenging Mr. Ling)

I will if you will.

INT. PARTY TENT—CONTINUOUS

Lulu brings organic lemonade to the kids and sucks one down
herself. Chilled water with cucumber and honeydew is served

for the adults. Waiters pass tempeh spring rolls. Everyone giggles and mingles. Lulu is about to slip into her guests' joyful spirit when she realizes that her parents haven't come back yet!

Lulu frantically searches for Alexis. She finds her in the pool cabana, tweaking the food buffet.

ALEXIS
Lu, check this out. I called Joan, mastermind of Joan's on Third, and made serious changes. So, surprise! Mac and cheese, sliders, AND French fries in silver cups. It all goes great with, ta-da! Your trademark chips and salsa, and your hyper-fave Garza-made tamales.

LULU
(beaming)
Now that's a feast fit for my friends!

ALEXIS
Couldn't celebrate Lulu without the right food!

Alexis beams with her fabulousness as a party planner.

LULU
(worry in her voice)
Look, Lex, everything's perfecto. But where are Mom and Dad? Ya know, I was just wondering about our strategy when they get here.

ALEXIS
(serious panic!)
Wait! Are you kidding? You don't have any plan for that?

LULU
Not yet. I can't get calm enough to focus because I feel
like there's a monster storm coming.

Alexis catches movement from the corner of her eye.

ALEXIS
(starts to scream)
The cupcakes! Watson's about to...

The tower of Sprinkles cupcakes crashes to the ground. Frosting
plunks everywhere. The pug hoovers up the yummy treats as fast
as he can.

ALEXIS
That stinky, pooping pug! Johnny! Where are YOU?!

LULU
(cracking up)
I think he's collecting his reward for stopping that cell
phone yesterday.

ALEXIS
Nothing about this is funny! What am I gonna do? I need
fifty cupcakes immediately.

Johnny Walker enters, wearing his spa robe, and surveys the disaster.

JOHNNY

Pug party!

ALEXIS
(shrieking)
This animal is outta control!

(to Johnny)
Can't you stop this beast?

JOHNNY
I think the first thing I'll do is get this pug's stomach pumped! Look at him going for the chocolate!

Johnny grabs Watson and begins to wipe him down.

ALEXIS
Isn't chocolate poisonous to dogs? Maybe don't go to the vet.

LULU
(gasps)
Lex, that's awful!

JOHNNY
Here's my suggestion for the cupcake crisis. Get that chocolate brown Sprinkles Mercedes van here on the double.

ALEXIS
Johnny! You're a genius!

Lulu is on her hands and knees cleaning the ruined cupcakes off the floor.

Alexis calls from her iPhone. After a minute she taps to end the call.

> ALEXIS
> They guarantee that within fifteen minutes, their cupcake truck, with all flavors on board, will be sailing up the driveway.

> LULU
> Hey, perfect. Everyone in L.A. eats off of trucks.

Elana sticks her head in.

> ELANA
> Girls, you do a nice job with this party. You work together to make something muy bueno. Everyone loves it. Hernandez is getting body rub! Officer Gale getting a manicure! I'm proud of you two. Now, go and enjoy the fiesta!

> LULU
> I think I better wait for Mom and Dad to come.

> ELANA
> If I were you, I'd enjoy now while you can.

Lulu and Alexis exchange a look then scamper off to join the party.

SCENE 9: MADDEST PARENTS EVER

INT. PARTY TENT—HALF HOUR LATER

The Spa-tacular is in full swing. Cheerful calypso music swirls around the party tent. The guests, who now call themselves Lulu-istas, bop, dance, or shuffle from spa treatment to food buffet in their slippers and robes.

Even the servers and spa technicians are enjoying themselves. The servers love watching guests try things like tempeh for the first time. The spa crew enjoys giving most guests their first facial, scrubbing, massage, or manicure.

Lulu, Alexis, and Mr. Garza sit side by side, waiting for their pedicures to dry. All three munch on chips and salsa.

> LULU
> Mr. Garza, I don't think anyone likes your salsa more than Alexis here.

> ALEXIS
> This salsa is supreme! It tastes great with anything dipped into it, especially these tofu skewers.

Alexis rubs a tofu cube into the remaining salsa.

MR. GARZA

Gracias, Alexis. Ya know, Lulu helped me make this recipe
better. Last summer she come to the truck and bring me
cilantro from her garden. We make experiments with the
salsa, and boom, it become perfecto!

Wide-eyed, Alexis turns to her sister. She's been learning lots
about Lulu today, like how she cleans up beaches from Venice
to Zuma and rescues dogs at L.A. city pounds.

LULU

Look, there's no salsa left, and my toes are kinda dry. I'll
go to your truck for a refill, Señor Garza.

Lulu picks up the empty bowl and heads to the tent entrance.

Exiting the tent flap, Lulu smashes right into…her MOM!!
Fiona halts abruptly. Linc bumps into Fiona's back.

All three freeze for a split second, enough time for Fiona's fury
to seep from her eyes and into every pore of Lulu's body. Lulu,
normally skilled at fast talking, can't speak.

FIONA
(trying to control herself)

In exactly four hours, Linc and I are supposed to be
on the Academy Awards red carpet in front of millions
of people.
(in an icy-cold voice)
And look at us. How did all this happen?

LINC
(usually the voice of laid-back charm now yells)
And what the heck is all THIS?

Linc waves his arms around, taken aback by the scene. A taco truck and cupcake van parked in front of his stately mansion. An enormous tent is plunked on his lawn. People of all sizes, colors, and ages are lounging, laughing, munching, and wearing white ladybug robes. And Watson, with his belly dragging, is running around naked!

LULU
It's, uhhhh, I know you're mad, but I can explain.

LINC
(exploding)
I said, what the HECK is THIS?

Alexis, who risks ruining her freshly painted toes, dashes from the pedicure chair right up to her Dad's nose.

ALEXIS
(sounding brave)
Well, Lincoln Harrison, I'll tell you what the heck this is. It's Lulu's birthday!

LULU
(jumping in)
I know it's also the Academy Awards and all. It's just that, well, it was my birthday first. I mean we, well, actually Lex mostly, planned this party before we knew. But honestly, it's all my fault.

ALEXIS
(strong and secure)
There is no fault here. Today is the day Lulu was born.

Alexis wraps a long, thin arm around her little sister's shoulder. Fiona and Linc stand dumfounded. They have no idea what's coming next.

ALEXIS
Fiona, you brought her into this world, and ever since then I've been the luckiest person because I have this amazing little sister.

Lulu is stunned and no longer afraid. She has her sister's protection, and more importantly, she realizes she has her sister's love.

LULU
Dad and Mom, I know you're probably not saying anything because you're worried that you won't be able to get ready for the Academy Awards. And it just so happened that your appointments, ummmm, were canceled.

Lulu and Alexis shoot each other sideways glances and try not to giggle.

FIONA
(finally speaks)
There are so many reasons I'm about to fly into a rage right now I can't even count them.

LULU

Well, let's just start with the time problem. You've gotta get ready to look glamorous ASAP.

FIONA

I was supposed to start getting ready hours ago!

LULU

Right, well, Alexis thought of that. Lex, tell her how we've got spa professionals right here.

As Alexis begins to talk, her parents remain frozen in confusion.

ALEXIS

Hotel Bel-Air Spa sent up their whole A-plus glam team. Oh, and we have an extra masseuse because Eve's here.

FIONA

Wait, did you say Eve is here?

LULU

Oh, that was a last-minute muy importante addition. Sophia's mom just had to be here with Sophia.

Fiona realizes that Eve, with her celebrity clientele, must have decided to give up thousands of dollars today in order to be at Lulu's birthday party. That's a lot of money for a hard-working single mother. As if pelted by hot coals, Fiona begins to thaw.

Fiona faces Linc to debate their situation.

Harsh tones and sharp words poke through Fiona and Linc's conversation. Lulu's stomach tightens.

When the tent flap opens again, Petal coolly strides in wearing a ladybug robe and butterfly slippers.

LULU
Hey, Petal!

PETAL
Happy b-day, girlfriend!

Petal takes a small box from her robe pocket and hands it to Lulu.

PETAL
Before I get a facial, Lu, open the box.

Lulu yanks off the lid and pulls out keys to the Escalade.

PETAL
I won't need those for a while.

Petal spots Linc and Fiona.

PETAL
Peace, guys! Relaaax!

LINCOLN
(sees Lulu holding car keys)
Does Petal think you're turning sixteen or something?

FIONA
(much calmer)
I think Petal just gave Lulu, well, ummm, us.

LINC
(still angry and jumpy)
What are you talking about?! What's happening here?

FIONA
(slowly)
Petal handed Lulu the car keys, but what she really gave
Lulu is our time for the next few hours.

LULU
Mom, Dad, that's really what I want more than anything
in the world! You guys being at my party has been my
birthday wish for—

ALEXIS
(cutting in)
Dad, do you even know how old Lulu is today?

LINC
(flustered and confused)
What? Definitely! She's...uhhhh...OK, let's think. Lulu, you
were born in...just tell me the year, and I'll figure it out.

ALEXIS
Here's the deal, Linc. If you get Lulu's age wrong, then
you and Mom stay. But if you get it right—

FIONA
(motioning for server to bring her water)
We stay. We stay either way. What an honor to be your
guests, because...
(pausing to control her emotions)
...Lulu and Alexis, I love you. You two are SO my girls.

Lulu and Alexis look at each other with amazement then back
at their mom.

FIONA
Who else, at ages eleven and fifteen-and-three-quarters,
could pull all this...
(motioning around the tent)
...off?

LULU
Oh, Mom!

Lulu wraps her arms tightly around her mother's waist. Her
mother bends down to hold Lulu in return, but not before
pulling her huge Tom Ford sunglasses over her eyes to hide the
tears that are welling up.

ALEXIS
(to Fiona)
Hotel Bel-Air's best spa team awaits. Let's get you
Hollywood glamorous.

LULU
And feed you the tastiest food to give you energy!

FIONA

Well, if Lex is in charge of the beauty and Lulu's in charge of the food, I'll be perfectly covered here. My first stop, however, is going to be Eve. It's been a slightly stressful morning.

Lulu, Alexis, and Fiona discuss where Eve might be.

Mr. Ling approaches Linc. Ling's face is red and puffy.

MR. LING

Excuse me, sir. I think I'm having a chemical reaction caused by my facial.
> (embarrassed, pushes his glasses up his nose)

Can you tell me where there's a bathroom?

LINC
> (concern in his voice)

Hey, dude, you really are red. Let me help ya out here. Follow me.

Lulu rushes over.

LULU
> (to Mr. Ling)

What's happened?
> (to her dad)

Mr. Ling's my science teacher.

MR. LING

Everything is fine. I just need to wash this substance off my face. It's starting to burn.

LULU

Mr. Ling, this is my father.
(gestures toward Linc)
But I'll show you where to go.

MR. LING

No, wait. This is your father? He should be so proud
of you.
(to Linc)
I've had Lulu in my class for three years. A most
inquisitive, intelligent science student. Always a delight.
Never a day of trouble.

Lulu's mind drifts from the conversation. She looks down at her
smudged polished toes. Absolutely, at this moment, her father
thinks she is nothing BUT trouble and that there isn't anything
delightful about her today, or most days, of his Hollywood life.
Lulu's thoughts are interrupted by Mr. Ling's soft laughter.

LINC

(noticing Lulu's curious eyes as she tunes into the conversation)
I've been telling Mr. Ling here that I agree with him.
You're beyond a fantastic delight. And that you've
never given me a day of trouble. Just a huge jolt from
time to time.

Linc pulls his daughter close. Lulu buries her face in his sweater.
This is the warmest birthday hug ever. She lets go of Linc after
feeling a tap on her shoulder.

MR. LING
Excuse me. The bathroom? My face is actually stinging.

LINC
(choking back emotion)
Hey, man. So is mine. C'mon. Let's go. I gotta wash
up too.

Lulu looks up to see her father's face blotched red. Before she
can study his emerald green eyes brimming with tears, Linc puts
his hand on Mr. Ling's elbow and steers him toward the house.

SCENE 10: PARTY WITH PERFECTION

INT. PARTY TENT—30 MINUTES LATER

Linc and Fiona have settled down to get themselves Academy
Award ready. Fiona's minimassage helped her unwind and settle
her nerves; now she's moved on to nails and hair.

Linc gobbles down tamales and chats with guests. Fiona makes
sure Linc's nails get buffed and his hair *coiffed*.

Suddenly, Alexis looks over Lulu's shoulder and lets out a shriek.

Sauntering toward Lulu is none other than Stab and his beautiful, gigantic girlfriend Slovinia, AKA GLAMAZON. Linc
calls out while getting his hair trimmed.

LINC
(smiling)
Hey, man, this is an exclusive party! You got credentials?
You on the list?

Linc and Stab laugh—a couple of boys messing around.

STAB
(to Lulu)
Birthday girl! Look, you've got it all going on!

Stab grabs Lulu and lifts her into the air.

LULU
(whispering into his ear)
Thanks for calling their assistants.

STAB
(whispers back)
Thanks for calling me, sweetheart. Nothing I love more
than messing up the order of things.

Alexis leads Glamazon into the spa tent.

Sophia shyly approaches Lulu and Stab. Seeing Sophia, Stab sets
Lulu down.

LULU
Stab, this is Sophia, my best friend.

STAB

Well, you must be incredible also, Miss Sophia.

Speechless, Sophia smiles.

STAB
(thick English accent)
I saw a truck outside with some brilliant-smelling food. Mind if I make my way there while Slovinia's not looking?

Stab gives them a big wink then heads for the Taco Truck. Jenna dashes over.

JENNA
(barely able to talk)
Was that who I think it was?

Sophia now drapes her arms around Lulu and Jenna.

SOPHIA
(smiling)
Sure was. That's Stab! You mean the Pop Girls didn't know he and Lulu are close?

All three girls giggle.

JENNA
Lu, maybe this is a good time for me to show you what I made you for your birthday?

Jenna pulls out her iPhone and flicks it to life. She soon pulls up Instagram. Lulu and Sophia huddle around Jenna to see.

> JENNA
>
> Ta-da! Your own Instagram account.

> SOPHIA
>
> That's so cool!

> LULU
> (to Sophia)
>
> Really? You think so?

> SOPHIA
>
> YES! My mom uses it to post pictures all the time. She said I could get one for my birthday next month.

> JENNA
>
> Lulu, will you accept me as your first follower?

> LULU
>
> Of course!

Jenna hands Lulu her phone so Lulu can "accept" Jenna.

> LULU
>
> May I borrow your phone for a while? Ya know, to take pictures of my party?

JENNA

Love it! And, hey, I know where ya live, so I'll get it if ya forget to give it back!

The girls laugh. Lulu takes pictures of Jenna and Sophia posing like they're doing dance moves.

Linc stands up from the stylist's chair to make an announcement.

LINC
(hollering)
Anyone up for football?

Linc tosses Lulu's new football athletically from hand to hand. It's clear he's a jock.

FIONA
(shouting from across the tent)
Linc! You just got your hair done!

LINC
OK, because I love you, I promise, no tackling!

Everyone laughs. Linc adores having an audience. Fiona loves seeing Linc relaxed and playful. It reminds her of his boyish younger self.

Stab returns from the Taco Truck with a heaping plate of tamales and chips. Lulu snaps a picture.

LINC

Stab, you in? You be the other team captain.

STAB

Oh, yeah. I love soccer, but I've always wanted a go at American football.

Mr. Garza, wearing his Taco Truck apron, puts his arm around Stab.

MR. GARZA

I agree with this guy. In my country we play soccer, but I've wondered what your football's about.

Lulu pushes the button and captures another fun picture.

LINC

My team's called Lulu-istas!

Party guests skip, run, or walk over to the great side lawn. Even the musicians march over, playing a medley of football fight songs. Stab, Mr. Garza, Johnny Walker, and Elana get into a huddle. Elana's beehive bobs up and down as she explains the plays. Sophia and Jenna carefully approach. Stab pulls them in to play. Lulu, Linc, Miguel, and Officer Gale warm up with the ball. Chip and Robbie join them.

Alexis pulls out her iPhone and snaps pictures of Linc and Stab looking fabulously fit. She points the camera on the sidelines and snaps shots of Fiona looking gorgeously glam, cheering Linc on. Breathtakingly beautiful Slovinia stands next to her, laughing and clapping every time Stab catches the ball.

Lulu, flushed and exhausted, runs off the field toward Alexis.

> ALEXIS
> (under her breath)
> OK, Happy Academy Awards Day, Pop Girls!

Lulu's eyes focus on Alexis's phone screen.

> ALEXIS
> (tapping and scrolling away)
> I want those wannabes to see what they missed. Tara Falls's pre-Oscar party fell flat. A big whoop that went nowhere. No stars showed.

> LULU
> How'd you know?

> ALEXIS
> It's already online, my behind-the-times sister!

> LULU
> Hey, wait a minute! Did you just send the photos you took to TMZ?

> ALEXIS
> Lu, I'm impressed you know THE hot online celebrity gossip site.

LULU

Hey, I didn't spend weeks marooned on Pop Girl Island and not learn something!

ALEXIS

Well, what Pop Girls are learning right now is that if they'd come to your party with Jenna, they'd have gotten their nails done with Fiona, eaten chips and salsa with Stab, and played football with Linc.

LULU

Lex, can you follow me on Instagram?

ALEXIS

(looks right at Lulu)

What?!

Lulu pulls out Jenna's phone and shows Alexis her pictures: Stab chowing down tamales and Mr. Garza and Stab grinning, arms around each other.

LULU

I've posted them but, I, ummmm, only have one follower. Jenna. And, right now she's trying to steal a football from Officer Gale—

ALEXIS

On it!

Alexis's fingers tap and bob faster than a rock star plucking guitar strings.

                         FIONA
                  (joining her daughters)
So fun!
                (stops and checks her phone)
I'm getting all these pings from my publicist saying the
photos on TMZ are the talk of Hollywood. No one has
a family like ours, outside playing football on Academy
Awards Day. Great photos, Lex!

Alexis beams at her mother's praise.

                        ALEXIS
Mom, please request Lulu on Instagram and give her a
shout-out. Oh, and then like and repost her photos. 'K?

                         FIONA
Sure. And should I repost them on Linc's Instagram
also?

                   LULU and ALEXIS
YES!

Within a minute, Fiona zaps out Lulu's photos to all her and
Linc's followers, who number in the thousands.

                         FIONA
Done.

Fiona puts her phone away.

FIONA

OK, it's mere hours before the Academy Awards, and I feel totally calm and relaxed. Incredible.

Fiona rests her head on Alexis's shoulder and grabs hold of Lulu's hand.

LULU

Mom, would you say that sometimes life's so lulu it's even BETTER than the movies?

Fiona's gorgeous face breaks into a wide smile.

FIONA

Well, I think my answer right now is that life can be better than a movie if you let it.

ALEXIS

Don't worry, Fiona. We won't tell anyone you said that.

Fiona tosses an arm around each of her daughters' waists.

Camera pulls back. Wide shot of football game, Lulu, Alexis, and Fiona, all washed in the afternoon sunshine.

 CUT!! I gotta say my mother and father hanging out at the party with me and my sister means the world, all the planets, the sun, all the stars, and the moon to me. Who needs L.A.'s famous Griffith Observatory? Return to ACTION!!

SCENE 11: A HOLLYWOOD ENDING

INT. LINC AND FIONA'S HUGE BEDROOM SUITE—SUNDAY 3:00 P.M.

Fiona and Linc dress for the Oscars. Alexis and Lulu zip, button, and hook their mother into a flowing, ivory-colored gown that looks spectacular with her up-do.

Alexis and Lulu look through their mom's jewelry. Lulu holds up a blue tourmaline stone necklace.

> **LULU**
>
> How about this?

> **FIONA**
>
> Well, the Oscars is a rather diamond-y night.
> (turning to Alexis)
> Lex, what necklace?

> **ALEXIS**
>
> (excited to be asked a style question by her glam perfect mother)
> Well, the envelope, please: DIAMONDS!
> (everyone giggles)
> Those blue stones are too casual. You have your own hyper-sparkling Cartier jewels Dad bought you. Wear these...

Fishing through Fiona's jewel case, Alexis pulls out a glittering diamond necklace.

FIONA

Lulu, I gotta go with Lex on this one. But, would you like this necklace as a birthday present? Here...
>> (hands blue stone necklace to Lulu)
Looks magnificent with your green eyes.

LULU

Mom, uhh, I love these. But, like, what do I wear it with?

ALEXIS

Well, not orange.

Lulu scrunches her face to pretend she's angry at her sister. She then cradles the necklace and thinks a moment.

LULU
>> (slowly)
Ummmmm, well, for my birthday present, I was gonna ask you and Dad if I could make donations to Heal the Bay, Save the Redwoods League, Audubon Society, and—

FIONA

Give me a list, Lulu, and we'll go over it together. We can support those causes as a family.

LULU

Well, I was also gonna ask about some money I need for an investment.

FIONA

Do you want to buy a whole forest?

ALEXIS

Or ocean?

LULU

No, a taco truck! You see, Señor Garza needs money to
keep his truck. Things haven't been so great lately.

Linc overhears the conversation, having walked into Fiona's
dressing area. His bowtie hangs undone around his neck.

LINC

Done!

FIONA

No, you're not done. Your tie!

LINC

I mean, Garza's truck. Lulu already saved it.

All stare at him. He acts like he doesn't notice but then lets his
face erupt into a huge smile.

LINC

Seems three women in this room have been posting
pictures of Stab eating food from the Taco Truck.

LULU

You mean my pictures?! The ones I took?

LINC

Yup. Those pictures have been flying all over the world!

In the last hour, Mr. Garza has had so many requests for everything from food to interviews, he and Miguel are the newest L.A. food celebrities!

Lulu dashes to her dad, but he holds up his hand.

LINC

Lulu, don't come any closer. Your mother's gonna kill me if I get messed up or smell like cilantro, garlic, and onion.

Linc and Lulu laugh. Fiona comes over and ties her husband's bow tie.

LINC
(affectionately to his wife)

Nice necklace.

ALEXIS
(to Fiona)

Wearing a necklace Linc bought you does make you extra cool. You might be the only lady at the Awards tonight who actually owns her jewelry.

LULU

What do you mean? Is everyone else there a jewel thief?

FIONA

Lex, you might be right.
(to Lulu)
Any star who might be photographed on the red carpet is given clothes, shoes, and jewels to wear to the Oscars.

All the top designers want a famous person to wear their creations in front of the cameras.

LULU
Wow, for free? Why didn't you do that?

FIONA
I did. But you guys canceled my appointment with my stylist. She got so mad she gave my wardrobe for tonight to someone else!

LULU
How funny is that? Some star is gonna be wearing the dress and jewelry you were supposed to wear!

FIONA
(shooting a look at Lulu)
I didn't think it was too funny this morning.

HARRISONS' GRAND FRONT MOTOR COURT—3:30 P.M.

Petal sits behind the wheel of the Escalade. Reaching through the window, Lulu hands Petal the car keys, hugs her around the shoulders, then bounces off to sit with Sophia on the front steps of the house. The girls plan a super-fab Academy Awards night sleepover (Sophia gets to sleep over, even though it's a school night).

Alexis leans against the car. Her iPhone is already set to camera.

Watson slowly waddles over from the party tent.

LULU
Here comes the last party guest. Watson closed down the Spa-tacular.

ALEXIS
He smells like a mixture of frosting and salsa.

LULU
I hope he doesn't puke.

Watson trudges past them and lies down a few feet away.

The girls spin around as soon as they hear the front door open.

Linc and Fiona exit the house. Linc escorts Fiona to the car while Alexis takes pictures.

Lulu and Sophia call out "Go *Silver Water*," and "Go Linc Harrison!" Suddenly, a muffled cell phone chirps like a trapped bird. Fiona hesitates, then opens a beaded evening purse.

FIONA
(to Linc)
Sorry. I just have to. You never know.
(flips open a tiny phone)
Fiona speaking.

Linc imitates Fiona—standing still, head cocked, face serious, listening. When Fiona sees him, she smiles and playfully waves him away.

> FIONA
> (hanging up)

Well, that was good news.

> LULU

What was?

> FIONA

Lex, you're coming with us! That was the director of tonight's show who called me personally to say he got me an extra ticket. Just do a quickie glam-o change. Petal can drop us and come back for you.

In L.A.'s hazy, pinkish, late afternoon light, Alexis first looks at her mother with gleeful surprise then turns and looks over at Lulu and Sophia scrunched together on the front steps. Lulu understands instantly.

> LULU

Lex, you should go. How mucho cool to see the Academy Awards live! People all over the world will be watching. And you'd be there when Mom and Dad win!

Alexis looks at her parents, who twitch, eager to get going. Alexis places one arm around Fiona and her other arm around Linc.

> ALEXIS
> (looking at her mother)

No, thank you, Fiona. Très incredible of you to score me a ticket, but I'm gonna hang with Lulu, Sophia, and Elana. And Robbie's gonna come back and watch here too.

(to Lulu and Sophia)
Well, you guys did say something about making popcorn and plopping onto the comfy screening room couch to watch the Oscars, right?

LULU
Popcorn balls. We're making salted caramel popcorn balls.

PETAL
Hate to pull the plug, amigos, but we need to motor into the monster of all L.A. traffic to get to the Dolby Theater.

SOPHIA
So that Mr. Harrison can pick up his Oscar.

LINC
(soft, witty twang)
Well, ladies, popcorn balls could get me to skip out on getting any old Academy Awards. But I have a date with this drop-dead gorgeous lady here, and I won't cancel.

Fiona's laugh tinkles like delicate crystal bells.

Linc takes his wife's arm as they blow dramatic kisses to all. The girls blow huge, goofy kisses back. Linc and Fiona disappear into the car.

Lulu pops up, linking one arm through her sister's and the other through Sophia's. Lulu leads them up the grand steps into the Harrison home.

                          LULU
And now, the winner is...

                    (dramatic pause)
Lulu Harrison!

                         SOPHIA
               (pulls her arm free to clap)
Oh, yes!
                  (slight British accent)
It was a brilliant birthday! A party that entertained
guests from all over the world!

                        ALEXIS
You had an awesome birthday, right?

                          LULU
THE best. But right now I wanna make one more
birthday wish. Well, not exactly a wish. More like that
extra candle you blow out for good luck.

Alexis screams.

                        ALEXIS
OMG! That gross animal should have his mouth glued
SHUT.

Lulu and Sophia stare at the pug gobbling a hot, chunky pile on
the driveway.

LULU

Not even Watson chowing his barf is gonna let me forget
this wish. Ready?

ALEXIS and SOPHIA

YES!

LULU

Here it is: I want to write scripts that you, Lex, and Dad
can act in, and Fiona and I can direct.

ALEXIS

That's incredible, Lulu! You don't even like movies.

LULU

Well, it just has to be the right script!

Camera zooms in on the three girls laughing and then slowly
fades out.

THE END

Epilogue: Lulu's Wrap-Up

You *really* want to know: Did Linc Harrison win the Academy Award for Best Actor? Right? Before I reveal, I want to tell you things that are more important than an eight-and-a-half-pound golden statue.

ME

Today I did things I've never done. I wore a whoop-de-do dress (it made me feel like a grown-up), tried tofu (it tastes like a squishy worm), and played football (how are you supposed to catch a ball that has pointy sides?!). Trying new things with my family made me feel, well, part of my family.

MY FAMILY

It's not every day that you teach your parents something. Who knows whether it will stick, but just the thought that they may have learned from Alexis and me, THEIR KIDS, is incredible. It says lots about Linc and Fiona Harrison. We showed them that family is important. And perhaps, maybe it wouldn't kill

Mom to be a smidge more flexible and spontaneous. And it wouldn't sink Dad's career if he paid more real attention to what's happening in his daughters' lives. Hey, they're not going to remember these lessons every day, but even once in a while would be *muy bueno*.

I see my sister differently now. I used to think she was perfect because she looked perfect. But I figured out that she's like me in so many ways, especially that she wants Mom and Dad to notice her too. Having them at this party meant as much to her as it did to me. Our teaming up made her stronger, braver, and, well, *mucho* more creative.

REAL, NEW LULU

Here's what being eleven in my family is like. Next weekend:

1. Sophia, Jenna, and I are having a picnic on my new patchwork blanket. All the food will be homemade, including the salsa from my garden. My cilantro plants are thriving like crazy!
2. I agreed to go shopping with Alexis again because she agreed not to yank open the dressing room curtain. She's buying me a new swimsuit for my birthday.
3. Elana and I are baking a four-layer chocolate cake for me to serve at Dad's congratulations party because…HE WON BEST ACTOR!!

And, in case you're wondering, *Silver Water* won Best Picture. When she accepted her award, Mom thanked her "two lucky charms." She insists, however, that the congratulations party is just for Dad. Well, don't worry! Alexis and I are going to cook something up to surprise Mom. We just hope whatever we do doesn't get us sent off to a Swiss boarding school without snow boots!

Acknowledgments

Greatest admiration and thank you to my dear friend Ashley Palmer without whom there would not be *Lulu*.

About the Author

Elisabeth Wolf is a bit Lulu. She lives in Los Angeles where she grows fruits, vegetables, and native flowers. She bakes her children's birthday cakes and eats spicy Mexican food. Each year for *her* birthday, she asks her children, Philip and Emmeline, to give her the same present, "Turn off lights to help save the earth." But make NO mistake: she loves a good shopping trip and pedicure. *Lulu in LA LA Land* is her first book.